THE SUMMER
I FOUND YOU

JOLENE PERRY

ALBERT WHITMAN & COMPANY
CHICAGO, ILLINOIS

Library of Congress Cataloging-in-Publication Data

Perry, Jolene B. (Jolene Betty).
The summer I found you / Jolene B. Perry.
pages cm
Summary: Kate, seeking distraction from her recent diabetes diagnosis, begins
dating Aidan, a young veteran who lost an arm in Afghanistan, and the two soon
realize that they might mean more to each other than they first thought.
[1. Dating (Social customs)—Fiction. 2. Diabetes—Fiction. 3. Amputees—Fiction.
4. People with disabilities—Fiction. 5. Veterans—Fiction.] I. Title.
PZ7.P4349Su 2014
[Fic]—dc23   2013028441

Text copyright © 2014 by Jolene Perry
Hardcover edition published in 2014 by Albert Whitman & Company
Paperback edition published in 2015 by Albert Whitman & Company
ISBN 978-0-8075-8367-8

Printed in the United States of America
10 9 8 7 6 5 4 3 2 1 LB 20 19 18 17 16 15 14

Cover Design by Jenna Stempel
Cover images © Peter Zelei/Vetta/Getty Images
and Julia Davila-Lampe/Flickr Open/Getty Images

For more information about Albert Whitman & Company,
visit our web site at www.albertwhitman.com.

To Mike,
for saying yes to so many things

1

Kate Walker

"I just don't really see us going anywhere, Kate." Shelton leans sideways against the locker. He shouldn't be leaning, not when he's so obviously breaking up with me—even if his eyes are apologetic. My heart pounds, pushing a lump up my throat, which is going to be a problem when I have to talk.

Shelton's black hair is cut short. Perfect for a young African American guy heading off to college for great things. I think he took a picture of Obama into Super Cuts and said, "One day I want to be that guy. Make me look like him." He continues, "We're going to different colleges. We're about to graduate...you know."

Now I need to play cool. Save face. I mean, it's not like I thought we'd get married or anything. Well, my brain might have known we wouldn't, but my heart doesn't know the difference. This stings, burns, and takes my breath away. But I'm determined not to show it.

I swallow a few times, trying to get rid of enough of the stupid ball in my throat to answer. "Well, yeah. I mean, we're in high school, heading to college...I get it." I hate that I basically repeated what he said, and I still feel like I'm getting kicked in the chest.

"We probably shouldn't have gotten so involved in the first place." He exhales. "You know, with how temporary everything is at this time in our lives." He sounds like he's saying something rehearsed.

Now the ache in my chest is being replaced with something else, something that tenses my shoulders, my sides. I start to get kind of pissed, but I'm going to stay cool. What else can I do while standing in the senior hall while Shelton Ingram breaks up with me? I run a hand through my hair, mostly for something to do. For thinking time.

Wait. "What about prom?" It's in like six weeks. I spent half my savings for a dress. One I knew *he'd* like.

"It would be awkward. Don't you think?" His eyes catch something behind me.

I whip my head around to see Tamara smiling at him. A junior, long, blond hair. With the little bit I know of her, she seems ditzy and so beneath someone like him. As soon as she sees me turn toward her, she walks into the nearest classroom.

"Nice." I cross my arms as my eyes meet Shelton's again, but I'm determined not to make too much of a scene, not to let him see how much he's hurting me.

"What?" He raises his brows, which is a dead giveaway that he's trying to look innocent.

"If you liked someone else, you could have just said it." Why do boys feel it necessary to play stupid games? And it doesn't seem like Shelton, anyway.

He leans back. "That's pretty mean right? And…"

"And lying *isn't?*" I uncross my arms and have to stop myself from shoving him.

"We're not getting anywhere." He shakes his head and walks off. That's it. *Walks off.* We've been dating for over a year and I thought everything was fine.

I hate that I don't have it in me to scream and yell. Instead I take a few deep breaths to keep from crying, which only sort of works. I blot a few tears away.

Must keep busy.

I know I have work in subjects other than AP English (like AP Biology or AP Chem), but I know it's the only class I'll be able to do any homework in tonight. I grab my overworn copy of *As I Lay Dying*, and stuff it in my bag. The lump in my throat and my pounding chest have left me weak. Defenseless. This sucks.

"How aren't you more surprised?" I wipe my eyes over and over as Jen drives us home. She's my best friend. She should be outraged— like I should have been when Shelton and I were in the middle of *breaking up.*

"How's your blood sugar?" she asks, tossing her long, blond ponytail behind her. Jen has these blue eyes that actually glow, and they make mine feel like muddy brown. Just like her bright blond hair makes my pale brown even plainer. Jen's also always *dressed*, while I seem to live in variations of jeans and T-shirts. But we balance each other out, and we've been friends forever. And we're going to college together at USC in the fall. All those things are worth a lot.

Wait. Blood sugar?

"Really? That's what you're worried about?" I hate it when Jen's meticulous nature makes her sound like my mother.

"Only 'cause the senior picnic is in a few days, and your mom gets all crazy with the curfews and letting you go places when you come home and your blood sugar is all out of whack. I want to make sure you can come."

"Fine. I'm *fine.*" I hate dealing with shots and carb counting, and everything that comes with being Type I Diabetic. Hate. Everything. And I've only been dealing with it for a year, but unless there's some miracle cure, I'll be dealing with it for the rest of my life. Mostly I'd rather think about how inconvenient it is right now. A future with it is too overwhelming.

"Okay, so he mentioned it to Toby last night, who mentioned it to me this morning, so I knew it was coming." She cringes in the driver's seat as if I'd hit her or something.

"And you couldn't *warn* me?"

She grimaces. "My phone…remember? And I tried to find you between classes but you were totally MIA."

Right. She got caught texting me in class yesterday, so her parents took her phone after the teacher called…*Oops.*

"I gotta make a stop at my house for Honor Society stuff."

"Fine." I slump lower in the seat. "But I'm staying in the car."

"Because you're grouchy. I know." Jen smirks before stopping in the driveway.

I want to smile at her expression, but I'm determined to wallow in my sucky day for at least a little longer.

"Be right back!" She leaps out of the car and runs to her front door.

I slump in my seat and stare at her enormous, grey house. We're parked under the separated garage, and someone peers out from the apartment above. Our eyes catch—his blue eyes are pale, and I suck in a breath. The curtain drops and his face disappears. I didn't know anyone was living in there. We use it for late movie nights and sleepovers. It's awesome 'cause it's not attached to the house, and we have privacy.

How many late nights did Shelton and I have in that apartment? The thought sends another hard stab through my chest.

"Okay. I have that Honor Society Meeting at Shelton's house." Jen frowns as she jumps back in the car.

"Don't look like that. You're in Honor Society leadership. He's Mr. President. I get it." Maybe I should be mad, but that's ridiculous. They work together. Them and like five other people. I know this.

She blows her hair off her face. "I really need my phone. Writing down all my calendar schedule stuff in a paper planner is really getting old."

I roll my eyes. Only Jen would miss her phone for the *calendar*.

"Ready for home?" She pulls back into the roadway, so I guess it's good that I *am* ready for home.

"Who's in the apartment?"

Jen shifts in her seat, but doesn't make eye contact, which isn't like her. "My cousin's with us for a little while."

"Which cousin?" Since she's reluctant to share, I want info.

"Aidan?"

I think I met him once, but I'm not sure. He's a year or two older if I remember right. I'm about to ask more, but we stop in front of my house (which looks like a brown one-story toy after being parked in front of Jen's). I want to be mad about my day, but really it all still hurts too much.

I stand up out of the car and the world spins. Crap. My blood sugar probably *is* off. I'll need to take care of that before Mom thinks to ask. I had an almost pass out two weeks ago, and she suddenly feels the need to check ALL the time. Since I was in her car and ran into the light post at the mall parking lot, it turned into this big deal. Mom's telling me that I'm not doing a good job of managing my own blood sugar, which means I'm not allowed to drive until I do. Today probably isn't going to help any.

"Come on in, Kate!" Mom opens the door. "Let's get you checked so we know what you can eat!"

I hate her artificially bright voice.

So much for avoiding the blood sugar test.

"I'm not sure what to do about the car situation," Mom says as she runs a hand through her short hair. "But you and I both know your level was extremely high when you came home today."

I take another bite of chicken thinking *extremely* is a drastic overstatement. Dad will chime in any moment. He's a doctor and knows about this stuff, though I swear Mom knows more about diabetes after all the research she's done since I was diagnosed.

"Kate." Dad breathes out. This is his exasperated one. Breathing out is what my dad does.

"Yes, Dad?" I'm still not sure if it's good or really sucky that he's a doctor. Mostly, for me, it's sucky. Especially now.

He adjusts his wire-rimmed glasses. "This is serious, honey. You take shots. You give yourself shots. You prick your finger. I'd think all of these things would help you realize the seriousness of your situation." He tries to make his deep voice serious and authoritative, but Dad's too much of a softie for me to be actually afraid of him.

"Thanks, Dad." Seems like a neutral and nice enough thing to say.

"I know you're just agreeing with me. And I also know that Dr. Masen's going to ask you about online groups, or if you've gotten in contact with anyone dealing with the same thing you are."

Right. No way. Now I'm the one holding in my exasperated breath. "How's Deena?" My sister is newly pregnant, throwing up everything, and her husband not only works full-time, but is also a grad student. Hopefully Deena's life will take some of the focus off me.

"Oh!" Mom's smile is immediate. "I spoke with her this morning. She goes in on Friday to hear the baby's heartbeat! And she may come stay with us for a couple of weeks while Lane's doing midterms!"

Perfect. A puking sister for two weeks. I should probably be excited to help.

"Kate." Dad again. Of course. He won't be distracted by baby talk. "Maybe taking away the car isn't enough of a deterrent. Serious things can happen to your body without the right amount of insulin."

"I'm aware of the list, Dad." Words like blindness, diabetic coma, kidney damage, nerve issues...None of it feels real. It's like this problem belongs to someone else.

Their eyes are on me. I feel them. Searching my face for more answers or explanations or *something*. I don't want to think about any of this right now.

What I really want is a night like the night Shelton and I had when my parents left town. I mean, it wasn't that big of a deal, but it was huge to me. He came and slept with me all night. All night I rested in his warm arms and felt his lips on my forehead, and I suddenly understood why people get married. Who wouldn't want to sleep like that every night?

"Kate?" Mom leans forward over the table. "Are you crying?"

"Just tired." I push to standing and start for my room, and neither Mom or Dad stops me.

I pull open my bedroom door and the familiar pale blue of my room calms me. But now I'm on the bed and it was the bed that

Shelton and I laid on. I hate this, and have no idea how I'm going to handle school tomorrow with Shelton there.

2

AIDAN CONNELLY

I flip open my phone, but don't actually get a chance to answer.

"How the hell are ya?" The loud, male voice sounds far away.

"Who is this? And do you know it's like three a.m.?" I roll onto my stomach, stretching the sheets around me. Gotta be one of the guys. Gotta be. At least I'm in the apartment over the garage instead of in my uncle's house where my phone would have woken everyone up.

"Hell, Connelly, you forget me already? Lost your brain with your arm?"

Fabulous. Arm jokes are starting already. Only Roberts knows me well enough to do that. I feel like an ass for not knowing who it was right away. "Hey, Rob. What's up?"

"What do you mean what's up? We're freezing our asses off one minute, hot as hell the next, and ducking when we're told to duck. You know Afghanistan. It wasn't that long ago you were one of us."

One of them. *Was.* It was like yesterday, but also a lifetime ago.

Three months.

Four surgeries.

Two hospitals.

One rehab clinic.

The apartment over my uncle's garage.

"Yeah. So, where are you now?"

"I could tell you, but then I'd have to kill ya." He laughs. Loud. He almost sounds drunk, but I know better.

"You guys still near Bagram Airfield?" I wonder if they're still close to where I was a few months ago.

"In the middle of fucking nowhere."

"No one," I correct.

"What?"

"You can't fuck nowhere."

"See? I knew you were smart. Fucking no one." He laughs more. "You heading to school? Everyone wants to know what you're up to, man."

"I'm..." *up to nothing.* I don't know what to be up to right now. I know what I *should* be up to. I should be getting ready for college, looking for a job. But I don't know how to do shit with one arm.

"Being a lazy ass?" he teases.

"You got it." Might as well play back, there's nothing else to do at this point.

He laughs again. I can picture him now, shaved head, pinched little weasel face always in a smile. And when he wasn't smiling, it meant he was about to pull something big. Like stealing all the steaks from the freezer before going on a weeklong "walk". Our first dinner and breakfast out of camp were awesome. Roberts is the best kind of guy to be friends with, and we've been friends since basic training. Since we learned we'd be in the same post. Same infantry unit.

"How much time you guys got left in country?"

"Four more weeks, Con! Can you believe it?" He sounds excited. After a whole year, four weeks feels like nothing.

Wow. "Sweet."

"Maybe I'll come to the great state of Oregon and find ya."

No, no, no. If I can't have the Army anymore, I don't want to be faced with it. "Where you stationed next?" I ask.

"I'll be back at Ft. Lewis, Washington. So I'm only a few hours north."

"Great," I lie.

Silence fills the line for a few moments.

"Have you seen Melinda?" All the tease is gone from his voice now. "You know…"

"I know who Melinda is," I snap. Melinda's the wife of the guy who died next to me. Two feet to my right. My body jumps at the black of the memory—the blast hits my ears making my stomach turn. "No."

"What about the, uh, funeral?"

"I didn't go. I was still in the hospital." It's mostly the truth. I was in the rehabilitation clinic.

"So, how's life with one arm?"

"Peachy." I need off the phone. I can't believe he just asked me that dumbass question. Rolling over all the crap I spend every second of every minute of every day trying to *not* think about is not what I want to do this time of night.

Though, I also don't want to be fighting away nightmares. No guy wants to admit to that. Well, no guy wants to admit a lot of the shit that's in my head right now.

"Look, tell the guys I said hi. I need my beauty sleep."

He laughs, again. "I knew it, I knew it! You're already going soft. Got a girl in bed with you?"

"Three. Night Rob."

I hang up the phone, reach around with my left hand, and feel the thick stub where my arm used to be. It still hurts like hell when I move wrong. My hand aches sometimes too, but it's not there anymore, and shouldn't be aching. Barely nineteen, no idea what I want to do with my life outside of the military, and now, because of the military, I *have* to live my life outside of it. Why the hell did he have to wake me up?

Aunt Beth and Uncle Foster are at the breakfast table looking at me like they always do—like they want to say something, but have no idea how to start. Aunt Beth is the slightly older version of my mom, and it still throws me. We all have the family blue eyes and blond hair, but Beth's hair is even cut in the same shoulder length hair as

Mom's, making them look almost like twins. I step into the massive kitchen and pull a bowl from the cupboard. Everything for me now requires multiple steps. Open cupboard door wide enough that it stays open. Let go of door. Pull out bowl. Set bowl down. Reach back up to cupboard door to close it. Pull open silverware drawer. Let go of drawer. Pick out spoon. Set spoon down. Close silverware drawer.

One damn thing at a time. Three months without my arm, and there isn't a second of the day I don't think about it. The thing is, no one in this house has yet to comment on it. Not my cousin Jen. Not my cousin Will. Not my aunt. Not my uncle. There's no way they're not curious. No way they're not at least a little curious.

Not that I really want to talk about it, but I definitely don't forget. It's not like someone asking me what it's like will make me suddenly remember I'm missing my arm.

"What are your plans today, Aidan?" Foster asks as he adjusts his tie.

"I'm not sure yet." I shrug, but it feels weird to only shrug one arm, and my shoulder's still really stiff. "I'll head to the pool for a while."

The swimming pool is what's keeping me out of physical therapy. Well, not out of it, but lessens it.

"You need my car?" he asks.

"Yeah. You can, uh, take mine today if you want." I love my car. Saved up since I was thirteen, bought it when I turned sixteen, and spent time on the thing almost every day until I left for Afghanistan.

It's a 1972 Chevelle Super Sport convertible. Grey with black racing stripes. The car is perfect. After years of scrounging through scrap yards and buffing out every fender, *everything* on my car is perfect.

He shifts in his seat. The words right at the edge of his mouth. I know it. *Why don't you sell your car, Aidan? You can't drive a stick with one arm. Definitely when the arm missing is your right one.*

Why couldn't I have lost the arm I don't know how to use?

I lie on my back and float in the pool. I know this isn't going to help me get out of physical therapy any faster, but it might keep me out of the shrink's office.

The pool is my safe place. No one here knows me as anything but the guy with one arm. They don't know it just happened. They don't know I haven't been this way for years. It seems crazy that I don't mind being somewhere that my lack of arm is completely on display, but there's no point in hiding something this obvious.

I have my stupid shrink visit tomorrow. *Recommended counseling.* Whatever. Like any one of those guys I go talk to have any idea what it's like to be walking out in the middle of the desert, in the middle of the night, knowing they're not alone. Like any of them watched their sergeant get blown up next to them, and felt around in the dark, only to find body parts instead of the real guy.

That thought sinks me. I blow out my air, and let myself drop to the bottom of the pool. My assignment this week is to think about what I want, and what I don't want.

It's all the same thing right now.

Sort of.

I rotate my shoulder a few times forward, and then a few times back before standing up and breaking the surface. My feet push off the bottom and I start a sidestroke. Left side down. The only way I can do it.

What I want:

I *want* to not wake up in the middle of the night in a puddle of my own sweat. It makes me feel like a fucking kid.

I want to talk about how much it sucks to use one arm, but not to someone who feels bad for me.

I want to sort all this mess out in my head about Pilot, his death, his family, and what the right thing to do is.

What I don't want:

I *don't want* the nightmares anymore.

I don't want to remember this forever.

I don't want to be without my arm.

I don't want to do nothing for the rest of my life.

I don't want to be pitied.

A loud bang and a shriek tense me into a rock, and I spin to face the noise. A kid, crying over a broken balloon on the sidelines as part of a birthday party, and me, ready to fight. I have something else to add to my list:

I don't want to panic over things that don't matter.

I want to be normal again.

It all feels impossible.

⚃

"Hey." My cousin Jen sits next to me on the couch, flipping her long blond hair over her shoulder. She's a senior this year, and is almost never home. Jen also got all the cool genes in the family. Her twin brother spends a lot of time in the basement with his friends and their games. I don't even try. You need two thumbs for most of them, and I'm a right-handed guy with a left hand.

"What's up?" We've hardly spoken since I got here a couple weeks ago.

"Our big senior picnic—carnival night—is this Friday. I kind of hoped you'd come?"

No part of this makes sense. I've gone out with her and Will two times. Both to the grocery store for my aunt.

"A *high school* thing?" High school was a lifetime ago. Two lifetimes ago. But really just over a year.

"Yeah." The word is drawn out enough that I know she wants to ask me more. And also that there's a catch.

All signs point to me not going along with this.

"No thanks." It's probably just a reason to get me out of the house anyway. I don't really need to be the guy with one arm back from war. I don't want to be dragged out of the house because she feels bad for me. I'm just not into it.

"Okay, look." She sits sideways and faces me. "I have this best friend—"

"Kate." She was probably the sulky girl who sat in her car the other day.

"Yeah." She smiles just a tad too wide. "You remember her?"

"Have I *met* her? The only person who calls this house is her and your boyfriend Toby. You know with the whole cell-phone loss and all."

"Oh. Right." She looks around.

There's something else. I wait for it.

"Okay, look. She's a big mopey pile of crap after her boyfriend dumped her."

"How does this concern me?" Not to be a total ass, but we're talking about some ridiculous high school drama that I do not need or want to be in the middle of.

"Oh, come on. You're not heartless."

"Again, what do you need?" I smile a little because I know I might be coming off a little harsh, and I don't mean to be. I've sort of lost patience with everything this trivial.

"Just another body. Please? I want to make sure we're even with girls and guys."

"You want me to go on a date with your best friend who's in high school, whose boyfriend just dumped her, because she's completely mental over their breakup. Is that right?"

"Um…" She chews on her lower lip. "Yeah? Only I swear it's not a date. She totally won't be interested in you, and…"

"Wow, thank you."

Jen's already flustered, and now it's kind of a game to see how much more awkward I can make our conversation.

"Oh, no." Her face turns red, and her hands start gesturing at nothing in front of her. "I didn't mean anything against you. It's that her and Shelton have been together—"

"I don't know." I shake my head. It all sounds so damn ridiculous.

"Think about it. Please?"

"I'll think about it."

Somehow between now and Friday I need to come up with a reason why I can't go.

3

Kate Walker

"It'll be a normal group thing. I promise." Jen's just driving all relaxed like we're going to go out for a burger or something. Not to a picnic where I know I'll have to face Shelton and possibly his new girlfriend.

I check my reflection in the visor mirror again. Ridiculously huge brown bug eyes, tiny chin, limp hair that we spent way too long on to make look curly, and a dress that I normally wouldn't be caught dead in—a pink T-shirt dress that should probably be worn with leggings underneath it. But losing Shelton has made me reckless. I push up the sleeves of my favorite cropped jacket. "Promise it's no big deal."

"Yay! And then if we see Shelton there, it'll be fine because there will be a bunch of us. We're not even riding with them. Will wanted to learn to drive a stick, so Will and Aidan already took off."

"Fine." I let out a breath hoping some of my nerves leave with the air.

"I still can't believe Shelton dumped you for a cheerleader."

"They're apparently not dating." I roll my eyes remembering his look of innocence about the whole thing. But then irritation begins to set in again. "Well, and his whole thing was *we're going to different schools*. She's going to be in *high school* again next year. How's *that* for different schools?" I spit out.

"Relax, Kate. Breathe."

I pull in a breath through my nose. So much for breathing helping because I've done one out, and one in, and I'm still a mess.

"Oh," she says as we pull up. "Aidan-is-a-bit-moody-and-lost-an-arm-in-Afghanistan." And then she jumps out of the car.

What? How can she have a cousin living with her for weeks and I know nothing of this part of it?

I leap out my side, and then have to smooth the T-shirt fabric of the dress down again to make sure my panties are covered. How did I get talked into this? Wait. "*What* did you say about arms?"

"Shh." Her eyes widen as I come around the front of her car.

Her gangly brother walks up with the guy who must be Aidan. He has the family blond hair and gorgeous light blue eyes. But he also has broad shoulders shown off by the snugness of his T-shirt. One of his shoulders leads to an arm. The other one does not.

I know I'm staring, because it's definitely something I should NOT be staring at. But my brain's having a hard time wrapping around it. It feels like someone's erased what should be there.

"Kate," she hisses. "You're staring."

"So, what does the other guy look like?" I grin at Aidan, and then realize I don't know this guy, and it was possibly one of the dumbest things to ever leave my mouth.

"The guy next to me, or the one who left the bomb?" His face is flat, but his eyes don't move from mine.

Silence like a thick blanket threatens to suffocate me.

Oops.

A corner of his mouth pulls up. "Teasing."

I chuckle this odd nervous little laugh, but both Jennifer and Will are silent, eyes wide.

"So, this is my cousin, Aidan," Jen says in this weird shaky voice that makes me know I've probably just screwed up, and that she might bring up my big Kate-mouth later.

"Nice to meet you." I reach out to shake his hand, but he doesn't have a right hand. So I stick out my left hand, and then laugh. This crazed nervous laugh thing. Again, like an idiot. "This has got to get old, huh? Bet no one knows which hand to put out." I smile and realize I might have again totally stepped over a line here.

"Yeah. I throw everyone off. I really should have asked to lose the other one." He smirks.

"Inconsiderate jerks," I say as we shake. But I'm sort of numb from nerves and hardly feel him, his hand, or the fact that we're done shaking.

His smile lessens a bit. And again, I'm stupid. "Something like that, yeah."

"So, Jen dragged you to our senior picnic." I'm flapping my jaws here, and I know when I'm like this I'm bound to say one stupid thing after another, but I can't help myself. It just comes out. "That sucks for you."

Jen flashes me a look, but Toby's appeared from nowhere and wrapped his arms around her from behind. I can't take my eyes off of Aidan. There's a lot there, behind his eyes, his face, something. He's interesting anyway. Well, and hasn't run screaming from my idiocy yet.

"It's okay." He shuffles his feet a few times and his eyes dart around.

"Really? 'Cause I think as soon as I'm done with high school, I'll never want to go back."

He starts to walk behind Jen and Toby, and I follow.

"Well, I wasn't going to come." He leans in. "But Jen said you'd make it worth my time."

I freeze, my heart racing. Who is this guy? And I'm going to *kill* her! "She said *what?*"

He chuckles, making these deep dimples in his tanned cheeks. His smiling face is such a contrast to his almost military hair, broad shoulders, and snug T-shirt. Someone as hot as him should be in an Abercrombie catalog or something.

"I'm kidding. She said that you would definitely be not at all interested, and she wanted even numbers."

"Okay. Good. She told me the same thing. It's just that I'm dating, or was dating—"

He holds his hand up between us. "None of my business. Doesn't matter. And she already told me."

I let out a breath. "Thanks." A small breeze hits my legs and sends a shiver through me. I'm so stupid for wearing this dumb dress.

We're all walking toward the boardwalk and the impossible-to-win games, and the same rides that have been here for forever. But it's supposed to feel different tonight because it's West Valley's senior night.

Only it doesn't feel different, or special, or anything because Shelton and I were looking forward to doing this together. To sneaking down to the lake and making out while our friends pay a fortune to win cheap teddy bears and stuffed pandas.

Our group has expanded to a few more friends, but I continue to walk in silence. I really shouldn't have come. Jen and Toby are totally absorbed in each other. Aidan is quiet next to me. His hand in his pocket. Weird. *Hand* in his pocket. It's just bizarre to not use *hands*. Okay, I need to stop thinking about the fact that he only has one arm because it means I'm bound to say something else stupid about it later.

"Wanna do a ride or something?" he asks.

I'd love to. But I glance down at the mini-dress I'm wearing. And even though it's all soft and T-shirty, it's not going to cover anything on most of the rides. "I don't do rides." I really should have put my foot down and opted for short shorts instead. I'm just not being smart.

I look up, and my heart hits the floor.

Shelton. Still looking like the token black model for J.Crew. Who wears designer jeans, leather shoes, and a T-shirt that matches his button up to a freaking carnival? Oh. Tamara's behind him, still in her stupid red, black, and white uniform. Who do they even cheer for this time of year, *soccer*? And how is it possible that there was nowhere for her to change. Right. She probably wanted to dance around in her uniform all night.

Gag.

Shelton's eyes hit mine long enough that I know he saw me, but he doesn't react. Just then Tamara screams about something and grabs his arm.

Pathetic.

I'm still staring, unable to look somewhere else, and our eyes meet this time. I really shouldn't have still been watching. His face pulls into something like a smile/frown. I don't care what I call it. It looks apologetic. Just that simple thing sends a rush of anger through me. But then my eyes float down his arms to his hands, his lean frame. His arms around me. His breath in my hair. The way his lips trailed softly down the side of my neck.

My body relaxes into the memory until I remember how he totally blind-sided me with our breakup.

"Who's that?" Aidan asks.

"Sorry, what?"

The guy next to me snaps me back to reality.

I'm on the side with no arm. At least it's distracting.

"Who's the guy staring at you?"

He's staring? That's good. I whip around, just as Shelton turns away. Maybe he was thinking something like I was. How nice we are together. How warm we are together.

Tamara sidles up next to him. He smiles down at her, and the way he's looking at her is the way he used to look at me. Like I was the only girl in the world. My chest caves, and I'm seriously ready to get out of here.

"Let's ride the Ferris wheel." I step around and grab Aidan's hand, pulling him into line.

"I thought you didn't do rides." His voice is so flat that I have no idea what he's thinking, or if he's thinking.

"Well, Jennifer demanded I wear this ridiculous dress, so yeah. No rides. This seems harmless enough."

His eyes flit down my body, and I feel even more naked than before.

"Ah. The dress is for the guy I'm guessing."

Aidan's smile is friendly and helps me finally take a deep breath in. I didn't even know I wasn't really breathing until I give my body air.

"I don't know about that guy, Kate," he teases. "He looks like kind of a wannabe *something*."

This is exactly what I need right now.

Aidan elbows me once gently, his soft smile turning to a grin. "Like he's trying *waaay* too hard."

And I'm still staring at the back of Shelton's head while Tamara finds any and every excuse to touch him. "He's neat. I know. But I kind of liked that, you know? And he's smart. Way smart. He's off to Princeton."

"Wow." Aidan nods. "That's a college I've heard of."

Of course. *"Everyone* knows Princeton. And..." He has real goals. Good ones. We talked about it. Together. I'm about to get all serious talking to Aidan. And who on earth would want to hear this? "Wait. You don't go out 'cause of your arm? Aren't there loads of people out in the world missing arms and legs and using wheelchairs and stuff?"

"Doesn't feel like it."

My chest sinks. Yeah, it doesn't feel like I'm one of millions with diabetes either. I definitely feel like the only high school girl who carries insulin around in her oversized purse.

Aidan hands over our tickets and reaches his hand out help me on. His hand is rough, strong. Right. Army. And again, hand. Not hands. Hand. It has to be really inconvenient. Actually, the whole thing is probably pretty horrific. No way I'm asking how it happened. I check his profile. Nice nose, the same perpetually tanned skin and dark blond hair as Jen. Soft-looking lips, hint of stubble. Nice. I wonder if he has nightmares about how it happened. Probably shouldn't ask that either.

I realize now that we're pressed next to each other in the seat that it's kind of personal, close. Right now I'm definitely not in love with the people that have turned this into the one fair ride of romance. At least Aidan's warm. It's supposed to be nice out, but in a thin, cotton dress that shows way more leg than I'd ever normally show, I'm freezing. At least I've left Shelton behind for a few minutes.

"What is it with girls and huge bags?" He points to my purse, crammed between my feet and forcing one of my legs to be pressed into his.

"We just...need our stuff." Okay. That was totally lame. I should tell him about the pharmacy in my purse. It's not like it's that big of a deal. But at the same time, he doesn't know, and that's kind of nice because I don't know anyone who doesn't know about my health.

"So, what do you do for fun?" His voice sounds forced.

"What do *you* do?"

"Swim."

Wait a minute. "But you don't get out much because you're missing an arm, and you hang at the pool?"

"Sometimes it's easier to pretend it's no big deal if there's no way to hide it."

Interesting. Still, I'm definitely glad I can hide my diabetes. I don't have to walk around with a stamp on my forehead or anything. *No, just a drugstore in my purse.*

Aidan leans forward on one arm, and then sits back up, like he doesn't know where to be. Then my eyes catch the back of Shelton's head until we dip down farther, and I lose him in the crowd.

"What are you thinking about?" he asks. Only he's caught me at a really bad time because now my brain is bouncing between Shelton, who has a new girl on his arm, and how Aidan does normal, everyday things with only one arm.

"How do you open jars?" I turn to face him.

"Um...you sort of put it all out there, don't you?" His face is unreadable. Is he annoyed? Does he care?

"Sorry." I push out air. "But I just say stupid crap. You've already probably realized that, though."

"I put the jar between my legs."

"Sounds like a pain." I do loads of things every day that take two arms. How does he stand it?

"It is."

"I can't believe I'm even talking about it after saying that stupid thing when I got out of the car." Jen seriously should have known better than to pair me up with her cousin.

"No. It's okay. I mean, no one ever asks. It's like they all try to pretend my arm's still there and it isn't. Seems like sort of a silly thing to pretend." He shrugs again, but this time he only shrugs the shoulder with the arm.

"Does it still hurt?" The words come out before I can think.

He nods once. It looks like resignation. "Like hell."

His answer is totally unexpected and makes my gut drop. I mean, he's out and about, hanging with my neurotic self on the Ferris wheel. "Sorry."

"It is what it is."

"So, you can ask me something personal and embarrassing if you want. Even us out."

Aidan doesn't say anything. Great. I lean forward and try to pick Shelton out of the crowd. My leg still touching Aidan's. I don't mind, but it's weird to be touching another guy's leg with my leg. But it's not like we have a whole lot of room on this seat.

I spot Tamara first. Her blond ponytail bouncing because she doesn't know how to stand still. Shelton gives her another look—the melt-a-girl kind. I mean, I know he's too far away for me to really know that, but I just do. I know it because we were together for too long for me not to. It's the look that used to jelly my heart, my knees, because I knew he wanted me next to him. What *happened*?

"You dragged me on this ride to make him jealous, am I right?" Aidan follows my gaze.

I rip my eyes off the Shelton-Tamara disaster. Of course he'd ask that. "And for the view."

"Why? Why bother? Why do you care?" *It's just high school*, he's thinking. It's practically all over his face.

"*Because.*" Because I deserve more from him. Because last week we were together and this week we're not and it doesn't seem fair.

"And the honest girl now feels like she has something to hide." He leans back, and I swear he looks smug.

Right. I am hiding, because we both know there's a lot more to my answer than that. "My head kept telling me we were in high school. My heart said that he's amazing and is going places, and I wanted to be with him. To be a part of that."

Our eyes catch and hold this time. The light blue is unreal, but behind that he looks broken. It cracks my chest further.

"People's plans get blown to hell everyday."

I don't take my eyes off him, but he turns and stares at the lights below instead of looking at me. My problems suddenly seem pretty petty and stupid.

The rest of the ride is silent. It's awkward, but not horrible. "I need to find Jen," I say as soon as we're let out of our chair. Better get home now before I ruin his night and mine with my mouth.

"I'll help."

I feel some warmth of relief that I didn't totally offend him. "Thanks."

With Aidan being just a bit taller than me, it only takes a sec to find Jen, and he waves her over.

"What's up?" Jen's breathless as she stops in front of us, her blond hair flying around her face.

"Can we go?" I ask.

She looks between Aidan and me a few times. "Everything okay?" she mouths.

"I just want to go home." Away from Shelton, away from the guy who I'm going to embarrass again with my stupid comments.

"When will your mom let you drive again?" she asks.

I shrug.

"What'd you do? Stay out too late?" Aidan teases.

No way I'm telling him what actually happened. "I dented her car. That's all." I glare at Jen so she'll keep her mouth shut. I hate going through all the stupid questions and dumb crap that come with having diabetes, and carrying my blood sugar tester and insulin shots, and having paranoid parents.

"Yeah." Jen smirks. "Kate's a *terrible* driver."

I narrow my eyes. Hoping she'll back off. But she knows me too well to take me seriously.

"Oh." She glances over my shoulder and frowns. Shelton is probably close again. Do I want to see? Do I not want to see?

"Yeah. Let's go." She puts her arm around me and begins to lead me away.

"Wait." I stop to look over my shoulder at Aidan. "Thanks for hanging with the crazy girl tonight."

"No problem." His eyes turn to Jen. "I'll ride home with your brother once I find him."

"Thanks," Jen and I say at the same time.

It was stupid to come here. Stupid to wear this dress, and I'm very sure that when I run over my conversation with Aidan in my head tonight, I'll really wish I'd stayed home.

"So, are you suddenly not telling people that you're diabetic? It's not that big of a deal." Jen flicks on her turn signal.

Toby's crammed into her miniature backseat.

"It comes with questions, and sympathy, and all sorts of crap that I don't want to deal with." I chew on my thumbnail as if it'll save me from feeling.

We ride in silence for a few minutes. "How do you think Aidan feels with no arm? It's not like he can hide that so he doesn't have to answer questions."

I hate it when she's right. "But, it's not like Aidan and I are going to be hanging out or anything."

"Well, he might be with us for a while."

"Really? Why?"

"His mom got remarried when he was in high school and now she has three-year-old twins and a baby, so there's no quiet and no free bedrooms. I mean, he might get his own place eventually, but he's only nineteen, and I'm not sure when he'll start looking."

"Oh."

"And he's just out of the Army and I think it takes some time for paperwork and disability and stuff to kick in." Jen shrugs.

Nineteen and waiting for disability money. Crazy.

"Did you two have fun?" Her eyebrows wag up and down a few times.

"Actually..." I try to think less about the warmth of his leg and his stunning eyes and more about his teasing and lightening my mood a little. I'm not ready to be *noticing* someone again. "Yeah. The night was weird, but yeah. I'm sure he'll never want to talk to me again, but Aidan was nice."

"Good then."

And I start to realize that my weird night would have been a whole lot worse without him. "Yeah. Good."

4

AIDAN CONNELLY

Will's driving my car like a pro. Must be all that training from his Wii. He shifts again, and it makes me hungry to *really* drive my car.

Just another reminder of what I'm missing, which reminds me of Kate. What an odd night. Definitely unexpected all the way around.

I don't remember high school girls being so hot. Or maybe it's that I was never able to get close to girls that hot while I was in high school. Obsessions with both JROTC and wrestling don't always go with pretty girls. Well, they might sometimes, but they didn't for me.

Kate. Legs, Kate.

It's the first time since this mess that I talked about having one arm and it didn't end in being frustrated or pissed. What a disaster though. A complete basket case over a guy who looks like...I don't even know what. Like he's trying too hard to be something I'd never want to be.

Reason number one I'm glad I'm out of high school. No drama. The way she watched him. Who would give someone power over them like that? Crazy. Stupid.

The chances of seeing her again are slim, and the chances of him taking her back are pretty good. My guess is that Kate is this good girl, and he wanted to sample something else, but he'll go back. I should pass on to Jen that she should tell Kate to ignore him. That'll probably work. Or, if she keeps wearing short skirts...that could turn him too. It definitely had me distracted.

"Thanks for letting me drive," Will says as we pull up to the house.

"Well, we both know I didn't have much of a choice." I reach my hand out and he drops the keys in.

His eyes turn down, and he gets out of the car without another word.

Should it really be this big of a deal if I'm the one to bring it up? Hell, maybe I am more of a freak than I want to be.

I watch Will walk his gangly body up the front steps to the door as I slump in the passenger's seat. My hand rests on the stick shift. As stupid as it is, I'm not ready to give up my car. Not yet.

Now I go through the process of getting out of the car. Unbuckle belt. Open door. Push door until it can stay open on its own. It's all things that with two hands roll along, and with one, don't. I climb the steps to my small apartment above the garage. My aunt and uncle were nice to let me use it, but I've got to start paying rent. Or doing something. Probably. Right now I just need to make sure I stay up late enough that I'm too tired to dream.

It's dark. My heart bangs so loud I'm having a hard time hearing whispered orders. I want to ask for a repeat, but I'd get my ass busted. The voice giving orders is too quiet. The dirt's in everything, and I'm lying in it now. Weapon at ready. Squinting into the blackness. Wishing I knew what the hell I'm supposed to do. A few shots pop in my ears, and even though there's only eight of us, I'm not sure if the shots are from one of us. Or them.

I re-grip my weapon. I re-grip it again. Focus. Breathe.

All hell breaks loose. Shots. Fire. Grenade. Bullets slam into my body from all directions. All I can think about is how I need to get the guys out, but bullets keep hitting me, and I can't move fast enough to help anyone.

I gasp for air as I sit up, my one arm hitting my torso over and over to check for holes. It takes me a minute to remember why both hands aren't checking me over. Holy. Shit. I try to just breathe while the room comes into focus and I remember where I am. My eyes scan the beige room. Wood dresser. Wood desk. Large wooden framed bed.

I'm in Uncle Foster's garage. Not in the desert. This blows. I'm now having dreams about things that never happened. The clock shows three in the morning, and the chances of me getting any more sleep tonight are nil.

"How are things?" Captain Daniels asks as I sit in his office. He's National Guard and probably thinks he's doing me some great favor by putting aside his private practice for a couple days a month to help poor guys like me.

"Fine, I guess." I slide down in my chair, trying to look more relaxed than I am. In reality my heart's pounding too hard, my breathing feels funny, and I'm just in an office, sitting across from some guy, trying to recover from another night of not enough sleep.

"Fine. You Guess," he repeats back flatly.

"Yep." Only I don't want to be here. So in that sense, I'm completely not fine.

"Sleeping?"

"Sometimes." I'm not at all ready to tell him that I don't want to sleep. Sleep brings back memories of things I don't want to think about, only they're worse in dreams because the reality shifts. And the more I dream, the more the dreams taint my real memories, and the more horrible my actual memories become.

"How'd you do with your assignment?"

"Don't make it sound like school," I say. I hate this room. I hate the white brick walls. I hate his pictures, and his diplomas. Everything.

"Don't *make* it school." He crosses his legs.

It's weird to see a guy in uniform crossing his legs in any way that doesn't involve a foot or ankle being rested on a knee. He's doing the girl leg cross. Not the guy one.

"How you doing on the job front? School?"

"I did my assignment," I say, hoping to change the subject.

That suddenly feels safer than the list I know he's about to run through.

"And?" He sits back farther in his chair like he's relaxing, about to watch his favorite sports team or something. It puts me on edge. I'm not here for his entertainment.

"It's all muddy. Everything I want has something attached to it that I don't want. The assignment doesn't make sense." I want to fold my arms across my chest, but there's no way to do that with only one.

"Well, then you took it seriously. Why don't you start with something easy." He brings a hand to his chin. Sometimes I wonder if he practices ways of looking sympathetic while staring into a mirror.

Brilliant. I smile. "I *want*...the hell out of here."

"I walked into that one. Didn't I?" He grins. I have no idea if it's genuine or not. I never know.

"Yes, sir."

"Been out with friends at all?"

Oh. Right. This actually makes me glad once again that I went out. "Yeah. My cousin dragged me out."

"How was that?"

"Not bad. Talked with..." I suddenly don't want to tell him it's a girl. "Some guy. A friend of my cousin's. Anyway. He didn't seem bothered that I don't have an arm you know? Was just curious."

Kate rambled about the oddest crap—jars, missing it, and her dumb joke about what does the other guy look like. But I didn't even mind because we were talking about it. She wasn't trying to pretend that my life is anything like normal.

"And your aunt and uncle?"

"Still weird." I try to look out the window, but he has his blinds almost all the way closed. Probably because all I want to do in here is stare out the window.

"I've suggested this before. You could bring them in, or your mom."

I push out a chuckle in hopes he doesn't see that even if they wanted to come, there's no way I want them here. Sucks enough for me. "Mom's got her hands full with her second family, and my aunt and uncle work. It's not important."

He writes down a few notes. I hate it when he does that. I wish for X-Ray vision, even though reading a dumb doctor's note seems like a pretty ridiculous waste of a superpower.

"Have you been to John Pilot's house?" he asks.

My stomach twists tight, threatening to make me lose my lunch and cut off my air supply. "No. I mean, I *mean* to." This is the last thing I want to talk about.

"I believe his wife and son are living with her parents, not too far from here."

"Yeah. I think I knew that." I know exactly where she is, but I can't face her. My sergeant's wife. Can't. They got married young. She got pregnant. He freaked and joined the Army. Wasn't sure if he'd stay in, but they needed the money and needed the medical. I wanted in. I wanted that life, and now I'm the guy he should be. One arm is better than dead. Way better than dead. And it's not like I want to die, or wanted to, it's that I was the single, cocky guy out there, and I was the one who lived. It doesn't make any sense.

"You're deep in thought. Care to share?"

"Nope." I rest my left foot across my right knee. The way a guy *should* cross his legs. Better.

"I really want to see you doing something to move forward. You could get in touch with the Wounded Warrior Project. They have some great programs, people...I know you need time to heal up, and I know nothing's easy right now, but the longer you stay in the same place, the harder it's going to be for you to move past this."

"Past what exactly? The fact that I lost my arm? My friend? My career? Wanna pick one or should I?" I push to standing. "I'll see you next week."

"Soldier, you haven't been excused."

"I don't give a shit, Captain. The Army doesn't call me a soldier anymore. They call me a veteran, and I'm taking my wounded ass out of here." I step out of his office and head for the door, air, and my uncle's car.

❖

I'm sure Mom's house won't improve my shitty day, but I know she's worried about me, and feels bad that her life is so crazy. We don't see each other very often. Her new husband, Stan, works hard as a manager at Home Depot, but doesn't make a lot. They have three small kids, my half brothers and sister, and a very tiny house.

"Aidan." She smiles wide as she opens the door. Same blond as Jen, Will, Aunt Beth, and me. But there are dark circles under her eyes. They probably match mine.

"Hey, Mom."

"Sorry." She looks down at her old college sweats. "I'm a mess. Trey isn't sleeping well. I finally got him to sleep, but the twins have stopped taking naps…"

"I just. I was on post, and thought I'd drop in on my way back to Aunt Beth's house." But I don't know if I just walk in or what. This isn't the house I grew up in. Mom lost that when Dad died. Got Alzheimer's way young and was gone in two years. I was thirteen. When a guy loses his dad at an age he needs him most, he either gets pissed at the world, or he learns to accept the shit life throws at him. If it weren't for Mom, I'd be the first kind of guy. And maybe I still am in some ways.

The memory of Dad still pushes into me, making it hard to breathe. I don't have a lot of hope of ever forgetting Afghanistan the way I want to, when after seven years, losing him still hurts this much.

"Come in," she whispers. "The twins are…"

At that moment I hear a baby's cry from down the hall.

Mom's neck goes slack and she stares at the ceiling. "I swear, that boy…"

"I'll get him." I slide my shoes off and start into the house.

"Can you…I mean…"

I turn to see Mom's face redden.

"You've *held* him before. It's getting him out…" she stammers.

"He's a baby, Mom. I can get him." I hope. It's not something I gave a lot of thought to when I offered.

"Mom!" Lily cries from the kitchen. "Gracen dropped the applesauce!"

"Aidan." Mom rests a hand on my arm. "I'm glad you stopped in." But there's too much worry on her face for me to just take the nice gesture.

I move up the hall, step into Trey's room and he's settled back into sleep.

I'm relieved because now that I'm looking at him and his crib, I think getting him out on my own would be tricky.

"I'm sorry, I'm sorry." Mom bustles in whispering. "He just does that sometimes. Come on." She holds the door open, and takes my arm as we walk back up the hall. "The twins are watching Dora, so we should have at least twenty minutes for you to catch me up on stuff."

"Oh, great." I don't mean to sound like a jerk, but after going to the shrink, and spending another morning under the watchful eyes of my aunt and uncle, I'm on edge.

"Fine. *You* pick something. One thing to share with your old mom." She laughs totally unbothered by my reluctance to talk.

No one would ever think she was my mom. She's too young. She had me when she was sixteen, and she made it. Put herself through school and took care of me. My birth dad bailed a long time ago, and I don't know that we've ever heard from him. My dad was the guy Mom married at eighteen. He was twenty-four, and I was two. He's the only dad who counts.

The new guy, Stan, is just Mom's husband. They didn't get married till after the twins were born when I was almost seventeen. I was in basic training a year after their wedding, and spent very little time at home during that year. He's still the stranger married to my mom.

Mom sits in the middle of the couch, and pats the seat next to her. I flop down and let myself relax.

"I...uh..." I have no idea what to share.

"Been out at all? More swimming pool, more wishing you didn't have to go see the dink that's your counselor," she teases.

"I went out the other night," I say, and immediately think about Kate.

"Oh." She pushes a finger into my cheek. "You can't hide that face from me. Tell me about her."

"It's not like that, Mom." But I can't look Mom in the eyes. It feels like such a juvenile reaction over a girl that I don't like.

"Uh..." she teases. "I think it is exactly like that."

"I was asked by Jen to hang with her friend Kate."

"I've met Kate. She's a pretty, smart girl. I thought she was dating someone?"

"She was."

"What's she like?" Mom's smile is soft, and all her attention is on me, even though I know that part of her probably really wants a nap.

"Pretty. A bit odd." I stare at my lap remembering our night.

"Which I think you like a little more than you want to admit," she says.

"I don't know. Anything normal feels so many miles away right now." I sigh and sag farther into the couch.

Mom rubs her hand across my chest a few times. "But that normal is what's going to make you feel better again. You know that, right?"

"Yeah." I nod. "I guess I know that."

"You're just agreeing. Tell me what you're thinking." Mom touches the small scars on my neck and around my ear—footprints of shrapnel.

"That even *if* I felt that way about Kate, she doesn't feel that way about me." No way. She's young and does ridiculous things like dressing up in something she hates to get the attention of some guy who's dating someone else.

"Are you sure?"

"I saw the ex, am related to her best friend, so I have some idea of her type, Mom." After seeing Shelton, there's no way she'd go for a guy who has no interest in moving beyond jeans and white T-shirts, and has no idea what to do with his life.

"Well, I'm glad you came. I know it has to be weird for you here, and I still feel bad that I'm not set up better, you know, for you to stay." She rests her head on the back of the couch and looks at me way too closely, the way she always has.

"It's okay. I feel like I have my own place, you know? It's good." But I only sort of have my own place, and I don't feel right living there rent free, but I'm not sure how to go about fixing that just yet.

"Good." Her hand drops down from my scars.

"And I know I need to sell my car. Uncle Foster's been really nice about letting me drive his. All the guys at his work are drooling over mine."

Mom laughs. "Of course they are. They're accountants."

"I guess."

"Aidan?" She waits until my eyes are squarely on hers. "You don't have to do anything until you're ready. As long you keep moving forward, I don't care how slow it is. I only want to make sure you're not sliding back."

That makes two of us.

5

Kate Walker

I can't concentrate in school. I can't concentrate at home. I forget
that I'm supposed to be mad about not driving, and stop rolling my
eyes at Mom when she checks my blood sugar the moment I walk
in the door from school. The lack of snark in my life for the past
two weeks is starting to be disturbing, but I'm not sure if I have it
in me to care.

I'm reading way ahead in English now, which isn't unusual,
but I am two books ahead, which means I'm halfway through *Alas,
Babylon*, and we haven't even had our Faulkner discussion yet.

Even Mom says I need to get out more. Jen apologizes for being
so busy, but it's near the end of the school year, and she's part of
prom committee, student government, and Honor Society. Why
does she have to be such an overachiever? I'm in Honor Society, but
I'm not running around like a mad woman.

Oh. And Mom announces that Deena will for sure be
spending some time here while her husband, Lane, does some
research or school midterms or something. She'll need to be in
my room because Deena's old room is mom's sewing room, and

then Mom laid on the guilt trip—*I know you're a good sister and won't mind.*

It sounds perfectly crappy to me, sharing my room with a sister who apparently is so sick she's throwing everything up. I know I sound horrible, and I love my sister, but the only thing she talks about now is the baby.

Toby and Shelton remain good friends, even though he's dating my best friend, and my best friend should hate Shelton on principle. Since Toby's dating Jen and claims to love her, he could at least be snubbing Shelton a little bit too.

But he's not.

Which means that earlier today, during lunch *my* best friend was forced to eat lunch across from Tamara, who looked way too pleased with herself about sitting all snuggled against Shelton's arm. I toss my math book into my locker and grab Faulkner.

Shelton leans against a locker next to me. Almost like he did on the day we broke up. His stupid gesture makes me want to scream.

"I didn't realize you'd take it so hard. Maybe I should have done things differently somehow. I don't know." His voice is filled with sympathy, making me want to curl up in his arms, or smack him in the face. I'm still undecided.

Half of me is pissed he thinks he has this power over me, and then I realize he does have this power over me, and then I look at his lips and remember how they felt on mine. I breathe in and he smells so good. He uses some ridiculously expensive cologne, but it's worth Every. Single. Penny he spends on it.

I half close my eyes and lean in.

"Are you trying to kiss me?"

My eyes snap open to see him leaning back.

"Screw you." I jerk my bag out, slam the locker shut, and almost run away to get some distance. *What's wrong with me?*

I'm not this girl—this weeping, whiny-over-a-boy pathetic girl. I'm Kate. I'm smart. Not terrible looking. Have some sort of interesting future...in something...

I need home. Out of school. I feel all uptight and strung up. Oh. Shot. I forgot. Bet my blood sugar is way high. I mean, when *I* can tell I'm a little on edge, it means something probably needs to be done.

And this is when I'm really glad that I illegally bring my own shots and testing stuff to school, because when my levels are off, the nurse calls Mom. Never good. I head to the ladies room, to the handicap stall, and wish there was a baby changing station in here for me to put my stuff, but I know something like that would never go in. The school board would assume we'd all run off and get pregnant just to have something to set there. Ridiculous.

I sit on the floor and pull out my stuff.

Finger prick first. And even after a year I still flinch even though it barely hurts.

Now I get to wait for my little machine to read my blood sugar.

I'm at two eighty. My levels could be worse. I mean, if I wasn't diabetic, it would be insane, but I've had much higher than this. I measure out the right amount of insulin, and try not to think about what kind of germs are on the floor while I lie down. I know. Everyone but me does it standing up. I just don't want to see it, and I swear it's easier to pull a pinch of skin out when I'm lying down. Now I just need to hope no one comes in. I pull up my white T-shirt, grab a nice little roll above my jeans, grimace, try not to think about the fact that I'm putting a *needle* in my *body*, and stab.

The small prick makes me suck in a breath, and I push on the syringe until I hit the end while a small tear escapes.

Forever.

I will do this forever.

It makes me want to scream and cry all at the same time.

I put the cap back on the needle. I make up a lower number, one hundred eighty, before writing it in my ridiculous notebook, and stand up. Yeah. I've had about enough high school for one day.

"No, Kate. I'm not ditching with you, and I can't lend you my car. It's my mom's car, and she'd freak." Jen shuts her locker and starts toward class. Toby's waiting for her farther down the hall.

Great. So much for my plan of leaving with Jen. "So, now what?" I ask.

"You can walk," she suggests, and then a mischievous grin spreads across her face. "Or call Aidan. He's home today."

She slips my phone out of my pocket and starts typing.

"Don't just call him now!" I reach for it, but she pulls away.

"Chill. I'm just putting in his number." She's furiously tapping my screen. "You know, in case."

"Are you seriously trying to set me up with your cousin?" I finally grab my phone from her outstretched arm.

"You're right." She shrugs, still looking smug or knowing or something. "Stupid of me."

I blink a few times, my phone in hand, but Jen's expression is still unreadable.

"Forget it." But as I step up the stairs, Shelton and Tamara are coming down.

I feel all shaky and thin, like I could shatter on the stairway if they touch in front of me. Have to distract myself.

I'm cleaning my fingernails, fiddling with my cell phone. Is that a split end? My heart flips, jumps, and speeds. Yeah. I *definitely* need out of here. I spin around and jog down the stairs, not at all caring if they see me or think I'm crazy.

After sneaking out the back of the school across the soccer field and around the track through the woods where the cross-country kids practice, I head to the road. I flip my phone over and over in my hands.

What to do. What to do.

Do I call Aidan? It's not like I really know him or anything. I flip to his name in my address book where Jen has added a few smiley faces where his address should be. Guess she does think it would be fun if I liked her cousin.

I push send before giving it too much thought, feeling more twisted up inside than I did while sneaking out of the school.

"Hello?"

Wow. He really does have a nice voice.

"Hello?" he says again.

Crap. I'm on the phone.

"Aidan?"

"Who's this?"

"Kate? From the other night? In the too-small dress?" He's a boy. That should jog his memory.

"Right." He chuckles. Then there's this pause.

"Aren't you supposed to be in school?"

"Well...yeah, but..." *Just get it out, Kate.*

"Bad day?"

"Kind of." And he doesn't say anything else. Have I made a complete ass out of myself?

"You, uh. Maybe want a ride somewhere? Or if you're looking for Jen, she's at school. With you."

Something about his tone makes me feel like I'm thirteen and he's twenty-five. My face totally heats up, even though we're only on opposite ends of a *phone line*. I totally wasn't thinking when I hit send. It's like, just because he's Jen's family doesn't obligate him to help me out. Jen didn't even feel obligated enough to me today to sit and eat lunch with me. "It was stupid to call you, I just—"

"You know that grocery store near the school?"

"You're going to meet me?" My voice gets all high and squealy-screechy with excitement, which sucks because I'm trying to play cool here. And I don't want him to get the wrong idea. It's not *him*. It's getting away.

"Only if you promise not to say anything weird."

Silence. I have no idea what he means by this. Is he joking, or will I be better off in silence or hitchhiking.

"I'm teasing you, Kate." He chuckles again. "Don't be so serious. Meet you in a few."

"Thanks." The word pours out in a rush of breath.

Something in my day is finally going right.

Time ceases to move forward when I'm waiting for someone. Ceases. Completely. I stare at my phone, flicking the light back on several times while waiting for Aidan to arrive. I shove up the sleeves on my short jacket again, and slide the strap of my bag between my fingers. My butt's planted on the backrest of a bench, and my feet are squarely on the seat.

My turquoise Vans are all scuffed on the edges, which sucks 'cause they're my favorites. What I want is a huge doughnut, but it means counting carbs, measuring insulin, and I'm not into it. Also Dad would freak if I tried to eat something like that—well, and

I've already gone high once today. Aidan already thinks I'm crazy. I definitely don't need to add to the pile with my finger pricking and insane-o girl diet.

Then I spot Jen's dad's SUV. I really don't need him to see me here. I start to jump off the bench to run into the store. Wait. Wait. I'm an idiot.

"Hey." Aidan grins as he rolls down the window. "Climb in."

I jog away from the bench and jump into the passenger's side, pausing as I take him in now that it's daylight. Last time I saw him we were sort of in the dark. His arm has that lean, muscled look the jocks have and his chest is broad enough that even his waist looks tight. Nice jaw, fantastic hair…

"So, you ditched," he says with the beginnings of a smile.

"Yeah. Guess so." I let out a breath of relief. No one I know. No one to judge. No one to say anything. Just a small intimidation factor at how super cute he is.

"You sound as relieved as I am." He glances at me briefly as he weaves us out of the parking lot.

"Relieved?" I ask.

"I was looking for an excuse to get out of the house. Foster's always looking at me like he's waiting for me to do something, and I have no idea what."

Wow. He's a guy and sort of got all personal. I'm feeling a bit flattered. "What *are* you going to do?"

He slumps and his eyes slide over to mine.

Idiot. "Oh, right. You're done talking about this."

"What's with you?" His voice is all relaxed and friendly like we're always hanging out like this. Not like I'm the weird friend of his little high schooler cousin.

"Same. Same. Kind of pathetic I guess. I swear I'm not normally this girl. I'm not sure why I let Shelton bother me so much. And I've never freaked out and left school." I can't believe how crazy honest I'm being here with someone I barely know.

He nods, but doesn't ask more. "My mom's family is cool, but I feel like they're always tiptoeing around me, and I hate it. If they have something to say, I wish they'd just get it out. You know how when you walk into a room and suddenly everything's quiet?"

My chest sinks. "And you know they're talking about you."

"Exactly."

"Oh yeah. I know that one." All my diabetes stuff gave me a good lesson on the whole hushed conversation thing.

"So, that's what it's been like." His hand clutches the steering wheel so tightly his knuckles are white.

"Gotcha." Wait. Starting really soon I'm going to need out of the house. Jen's busy, Shelton's occupied with someone else, and Mom's accusing me of moping. "Hey. I just realized something here."

"What's that?"

"You're not awful to hang out with," I say as the excitement starts to build. He is cute. And Jen's okay with us being together. And it's not like I'm looking for a new boyfriend, but still…

"Thanks." The corner of his mouth twitches in the beginnings of a smile.

"No, sorry." I really have to get better about thinking first. "I mean. This is safe, right? And keeps them off our back? Like we could get together sometimes to hang out?"

"I don't know..." Only his tone says he does know and the answer is no.

I feel a little prick of rejection, even though it was just an idea.

"You can take me home. I'm not far. I'm sorry for asking you to come." This was really stupid. The excitement of my idea just inverted itself into my chest. And not in a good way.

"You asking for a ride isn't a big deal, Kate. I'm just..." His eyes dart around a bit as he lets out a breath. "Planning anything right now is...hard. I'm not sure what's next for me, and I've never had that before."

I slump in my seat. "Join the club."

We ride in silence for a bit but it turns from the awkward kind to the okay kind pretty fast. I'm not sure what's different but maybe it's that he's not gripping the steering wheel as hard as he was.

"I'm gonna drive for a bit. I'm sure if you go home you'll be answering questions you don't want to answer. Wanna join me?"

His voice is unreadable. I'm not sure if he's just being nice, or if he's annoyed with me and is trying to cover. Right now I'm self-centered enough to not care. Hanging with Aidan in his uncle's car feels like the safest place for me right now—even though I feel like a bit of a moron around him again.

We get coffees—well he gets a coffee, I get steamed milk. Nothing added. He doesn't comment. I feel relief. We drive. It's quiet. I relax into the seat. We don't speak. I don't mind. He doesn't seem to. Better than me saying something stupid.

I feel bad for him because he can't even drink his coffee while driving. Each time we pause at a stop sign, he reaches for it, takes a sip and then starts driving again. It makes me wonder how long it takes him to do even simple things like getting a bowl of cereal. Giving myself shots suck, but maybe there are worse things.

For the first time that I can remember I just relax into the silence of being with someone who I think likes it as much as I do. But he is *really* quiet.

6

AIDAN CONNELLY

My apartment door closes behind me as I head to Foster and Beth's house for dinner.

I'm probably an ass for telling Kate I didn't really want to hang out. But the whole thing seems weird because her family will want to know about me, and Foster will probably give me some lecture about her, and it seems like we'd just be adding to confusion in our lives that's already here.

Getting involved with a girl on any level just isn't a good idea for me right now. There's nothing going on between us and Kate's already confusing the hell out of me.

But she is a cool girl. With really nice legs.

"Look, I'm sorry, okay?" Jen says into her phone as I trudge up the stairs to the main floor.

Aunt Beth said something about roast tonight, so I'm definitely eating with the family. And I shouldn't listen, but I do. No one can do urgency like a teen girl, and I'm curious.

"It's not my fault that I happen to still be dating the best friend of your ex-boyfriend."

Oh. Now my guess is that she's talking to Kate. Kate didn't say anything about why she needed to leave school early. Maybe it's something I should've asked. Or maybe it's good that I didn't.

"Why can't I call him your ex? One—it's been weeks. Two— he's walking Tamara to class. Every day." At least Jen's voice quiets down for the last line.

"Well. I just...I don't want you to be mad at me, okay? Next time it happens, I'll eat lunch with you instead of my boyfriend. Come sleep over this weekend."

There's another pause, and I stand in the stairway, knowing she can't see me yet. And also knowing she'll probably take off into her room when she can.

"Maybe next weekend then. Oh. No. That's the party. Look. Let's just make some time, okay?"

Another pause.

"Oh, come on. I can't skip. And anyway, Aidan rescued you in the end, right? He picked you up...Yeah, well, you're quiet too. He's depressed. I'd be depressed if I was him."

Right.

I really don't want to sit down with the family. Not anymore.

"I think I should call Aidan," Aunt Beth says. "I made this just for him. I know it's my sister's best meal. He's got to miss it."

"He knows, Beth. He'll come if he wants to come," Uncle Foster says.

Guilt branches out in my chest, and I know I'll be sticking around.

"Talkin' about me?" I ask as I jump up the stairs, pushing away all the weight that was starting to settle on my shoulders. I know I haven't spoken much. I also know they probably all think I'm depressed. Maybe I am.

"There you are!" Aunt Beth smiles her wide smile.

Jen runs for her room, phone pressed to her ear. I wish there was an easy way for me to listen to the rest of her conversation, but there really isn't. And I shouldn't care anyway.

Now I don't know if I *want* to try and apologize to Kate, because that'll really confuse things with me not really wanting to spend time with her, or if I *should* apologize and take her up on her offer because part of me *does* want to spend time with her.

I'm being ridiculous.

At least dinner smells good. I'll think about that for a while instead. But I can't, because I'm not sure if I hurt Kate's feelings or not.

Jen steps into the dining room, and definitely doesn't look at me. Right. Kate.

I slide my phone from my pocket and send Kate a text (not the easiest thing to do one-handed) before sitting down.

Wanna hang out Fri?

In two seconds I have a reply.

Prft timing. My sis comes to town that day, and I'll need out

I grin as I slide my phone back in my pocket, which means I probably want to hang out with her a lot more than I want to let myself think.

Uncle Foster cocks a brow, just slightly. Just enough that I know he knows I was texting a girl. Or suspects. I'm going to have to be more careful because I really don't need anything else hanging between all of us.

I get up more rested than I've felt in a month. No dreams, just good, hard sleep. Maybe I'll run today. It used to be my favorite part of physical training. I could time myself on the two miles to see where I'd fall on my PT test. I've always aced it. Always.

Uncle Foster bought me a pair of running shoes that don't tie, they have this weird pull string, and I'm suddenly glad. I felt like a moron when I first got them, but I don't know how to tie my shoes with only one hand. Not yet, anyway. I tighten them as best I can, and head out the door.

I'm going to have to hit the timer on my watch with my teeth as I take off running. I should be used to all this little stuff by now. Pants with one hand, buttons with one hand...I haven't worn a button-up shirt yet because I don't think I could handle the frustration. Even my elastic waist pants take longer with one hand. Everything is long, and slow.

I jump into a run at the end of the driveway, and this I can do. It feels a little lop-sided with only one arm pumping, but not terrible, not too different. The push in my legs is the same, so I *push*.

My lungs burn. My legs burn. I've run what feels like ten miles, twenty miles, but am actually still under my two-mile test. I mapped it. Just in case. It's been too long since I've run. The sidewalk begins to work uphill and I push harder, lungs scream. Legs ache. I push. My time is still good. I'm okay. When my place comes into view again, I really run hard. Fast like the wind. This is pain I control. This is something I know.

I nearly collapse at the end of the driveway, but my time's really good for not running in months. A few seconds over twelve minutes. Two six-minute miles. All I needed for the Army was to stay under fourteen. Easy.

Now sit-ups. Two minutes. I jog up the stairs of my apartment and use my teeth again for the timer. My feet slide under the bottom of the couch and I start. Up, up, up, up, up.

I forget to count and it doesn't matter, because I don't pause. My shoulder stub starts to ache with exertion, which pisses me off because it's not supposed to. It's a stump. It just sits. Something that does me no good shouldn't get to hurt.

"Shit." I stop when the timer goes off.

The throbbing spreads into my side, across my chest, up my neck and into my head. The damn thing shouldn't hurt. It's gone, done. I should be numb. All of me should be.

Whatever. It's not like I could do my push-up part of the PT test anyway.

I strip down in the bathroom—again, everything takes longer. Each movement sends another wave of pain through me. It takes all my self-control not to hit my good fist through the wall or the door or the mirror above the sink.

I imagine what it would look like—shards of glass flying around the room, and then remember that I'd have to clean it up.

The hot water rinses away the sweat, but it doesn't rinse away anything I care about. Time for some painkillers and a nap.

I wash a pill down with water I suck out of the faucet. I've hardly used any of the stuff they gave me. I hate feeling high, but today I'll take it.

How did I go from a good, easy day, to pain over too many things for me to deal with? My body begins to relax into the weight and my head swims. For a guy who's always kept himself pretty clean, this stuff really messes with me and I let my eyes close.

It's dark. Again. Why does everything shitty have to happen in the dark? Bodies push against me. My friends? My enemies? There's a blast and everything around me disappears, sending a ripping pain through my body. I'm in pieces. I'm yelling, asking someone to help me, and I'm somehow still moving, even though I know I've been torn apart. I have to get everyone else out of there. I start to pull on them, but I keep ripping apart as I do it. I can't help. The pain is searing, and the frustration and fear force me to scream.

"Aidan?" A hand on my arm. *"Aidan?"*

My head rolls to the side. "Uncle Foster?" He doesn't usually come in here.

"Hey. I'm really sorry for barging in. Your aunt saw you come back from your run, and she called a few times and you didn't answer. She was worried. And you were talking in your sleep."

"What was she worried about? That I went and killed myself in your apartment?" I ask. My brain is still all fuzzy, and my body's trying to recover from being blown apart in the dark.

There's enough silence to know that's exactly what she was worried about.

My gut clenches a little—maybe in guilt, maybe because I don't want anyone to think that's where I'm at.

"Look, Foster, I'd be lying if I said my life right now was what I want. And I guess I've been moody or whatever, but I'm smart enough to know that my Sergeant would kick my ass if he knew he saved my life only for me to take it later, okay?"

"You two were close."

Those four simple words hurt worse than anything I've felt in weeks. I can feel the beginnings of my body wanting to shake. Wanting to let go. But I don't. I don't have to. I don't want to. I rest my hand over my eyes, pushing my fingers into the outside corners.

"You want me to bring you dinner?" he asks. His hand still rests on my arm.

I open my mouth to answer, but I'm smart enough not to say anything. If I try to speak, I might lose it.

"There's a pizza on its way. I'll bring you up some, okay?"

I nod.

"Tonight might be a sleeping pill night, Aidan."

It might be. Though, I've slept all day, seems sort of silly to waste more hours tonight.

As soon as Uncle Foster steps out, I sit up and the room spins. Nope. Not taking a sleeping pill tonight. The stupid painkiller is enough drugs for me. It's just not enough to dull the ache in my chest.

Two in the morning, and I'm nowhere near sleep. Every time my eyes close, I feel the concussion of the bomb. Feel Pilot shove against me. See my own arm, or the bits left of it in the infrared, but Pilot...there was almost nothing of him left. Almost nothing to stuff in a bag and send home. Honestly I don't know if he sensed it, and pushed me, or if the boom from that thing shoved him against me. It doesn't matter either way, because I know he would've pushed me out of the way if he could. That's what counts. And I should've been able to do the same.

I want to drive, but don't want Foster to worry. I write a note and lay it on their porch. I still have the keys to Foster's Explorer so I climb in and drive.

As I head north, part of me wishes I wasn't alone. It sucks because I don't want to talk, don't want to discuss meaningless things, don't want to discuss meaning*ful* things. Just company. Just a person.

Now that I'm close, I know where I'm going. At least it'll be too early in the morning, and I won't have to feel guilty for not stopping in. Four in the morning, and I'm weaving through the neighborhood.

I'm embarrassed to say that I've come up here three times and never had the guts to knock. To go in. Tonight—or this morning or whatever—will be no different. It's safe to pause outside the house, so I do. This is when I see that soft, blue flicker of a TV. It tells me that she's probably as awake as I am. And probably over the same guy.

This was not a good idea.

I hit the gas and tear out of the neighborhood to head south. Back down the highway. Back toward the apartment that's turned into my bat cave. The place I stay, rest, and yeah, maybe hide. Beats the shit out of how I feel.

I turn on music, but two songs in there is one I recognize, one I remember listening to with the guys. I slam my hand down on the power button and then grab the wheel again.

The drive is long, but not long enough to erase anything, push anything away. I pull back into the driveway as Jen and Will emerge from the house to go to school.

Great.

I climb out of their dad's car and wave, like this is all no big deal. Jen gives me the weak smile that's just part of Jen, and Will tries hard to do the whole tilt-your-chin-to-say-hello thing, only he really is nerd through and through, so it doesn't come off the way he probably wants it to.

I jog past them up the stairs of my apartment. I'm not going anywhere else today. My night of no sleep is catching up to me.

Aunt Beth is on the phone as I make my way up the stairs in her house. I feel a bit like an idiot for coming in for cereal at three in the afternoon, but that's what a sleepless night will do.

"I know it's your anniversary, but Foster has this yearly benefit and I completely spaced out on the fact that it was the same day. Jen has an honor society thing. I'm really sorry, Christie."

Mom? She's talking to my mom?

"What's going on?" I ask as I hit the top of the stairs.

"Oh," Beth smiles. "Your son just came in."

"What's up?" I ask Mom as I take the phone.

"Beth was going to take the kids so Stan and I could go out for our anniversary, but it doesn't look like it'll work out. We can do it another time."

"I'll do it," I say before really thinking it through.

"Oh, Aidan. I'd love for you to, but three of them? It's a lot of work." What she really means is that she can barely keep up with them and how can I with my new handicap.

"When is it?" I ask.

"This Friday."

I grin. "Don't worry. I have a helper."

Kate wants us to hang out to keep her family off her back—she can come. Girls are good at babysitting stuff. I think.

As Mom and I get off the phone, I realize it might be kind of a big deal. To go with Kate. She's going to come and meet my mom. She might take it the wrong way. Though, it actually should be no big deal because Kate and I are barely even friends, and she'll get Shelton back if she wants him, I have no doubt. So, this should all be cool. Probably.

Another problem I'm now realizing is that Beth and Foster know her too. And she's Jen's best friend. It could really all blow up in my face.

Now the anxiety I already have over the stupid idea is going to stress me all week, making me wonder if it's worth it.

7

Kate Walker

"You so owe me," I say as I climb into his uncle's car. "I don't do kids."

He smirks. "You're the one who said we needed to get together, and we happen to be able to help out my mom in the process."

"Fair enough. Anyway, anything's better than listening to my mom and my sister, who refuses to lie any other way than face down across the whole couch. She says it helps her nausea." I make sure he can see my eye roll from across the car. "At least she's not checking my..." *Blood sugar.* But this isn't something I've told him. "I mean, checking up on me every few seconds."

"Are you still pining away for Mr. too-neat-for-words?" He puts the car in drive. "Or is that something I shouldn't ask."

I have to laugh. Have to, because that's exactly how I see Shelton. "No."

"Truth." He glances over at me with eyebrows raised.

"Okay, maybe." I'll give him that much, but no more. He doesn't need to know how it rips me up to see them together in the hallway. If he weren't with someone else, it would suck, but be livable. But he *is* with someone else, and it makes it so much worse.

Though, sharing a car with Aidan is definitely taking away some of the sting.

"Your sister sounds pretty miserable. Mom threw up a lot with the twins. It was my junior year of high school. Before her and Stan got married even. In my life before this one."

His face immediately freezes.

His life before this one—my guess is that he didn't mean to say that out loud. I had a life before diabetes too. One where I didn't have to give myself shots and count carbs in each and every single thing I eat.

Our night should be interesting.

"I guess I'm impatient with her because she's such a drama queen."

Aidan's mouth opens, and then closes, leaving a small dimple on his cheek, telling me that he really wants to say something.

"Just say it." I'm almost laughing because as awkward as our awkward moments are, the rest of being around Aidan is pretty cool. "Are you going to mention my ridiculous dress and Shelton? Or how weird the stuff that comes out of my mouth is, or…"

"Just that teenage girls, in general, are the biggest owners of drama there is." He lowers his face so he can look up at me with his teasing expression, but now all I see is lashes. For a blondie, he has really nice lashes.

"Well, I didn't used to be." Until stupid Shelton, and his perfectly pressed clothes, and perfectly laid-out future. And his stupid way of breaking up with me that didn't include him telling me that he liked someone else.

"Kate!" A woman's arms crush me. "It's so nice to see you again."

"Uh...you too." I stand back. Right. We've met at Jen's a few times. And wow Aidan's mom looks exactly like Jen's mom. I remember this now that I'm standing in front of her. I thought they were twins when I first met her. The reality of him being my best friend's cousin hits me again. This whole situation of Aidan and me hanging out could seriously backfire.

"You're so grown-up and stunning!"

Stunning. That's a word I never thought would be associated with me. "Uh...Thank you?"

"It's almost bedtime, so the night should be pretty simple. You have no idea how grateful I am to you two." Her eyes moisten up, and I want to elbow Aidan. I'm not the *only* person whose life is filled with drama.

She rattles off some instructions and I'm mostly looking between Aidan and his mom. It's easy to see they're tight. They stand close, talk easily with each other. And then it's over, and I have no idea what was just discussed.

His step-dad and mom walk out, and Aidan already has the baby in his arm. "Mom said Trey needs to be rocked to sleep, which I can do, but I might need help getting him in his bed as softly as he'll need to be laid down."

I step into the small, unfamiliar house. "Okay." I never know what to do with kids—especially little ones.

Two three-year-olds immediately accost my legs. I don't babysit. Ever. Kids are messy and smelly, and their little pudgy hands are always sticky.

"Come watch Dora!" The boy pulls on my hand. As Aidan disappears into the baby's room, I wish I'd paid better attention to the instructions we were given.

I sit on the couch, and immediately have a small child on each side of me. I'm going to be crushed, suffocated between two three-year-old squishy rolls of children with sticky hands.

"D-D-D-D-D-Dora!" They both sing with the show.

Okay, Kate. Breathe. They're just kids. They can't be that sticky and dirty. This is totally not a big deal. Aidan seemed perfectly fine holding that tiny, squirmy baby with only one arm. Crazy.

How long am I supposed to give him to put the baby to sleep? Great. It's not like he can yell out when he's ready for help.

"Tico!!" The little boy points to the TV and laughs. And then the little girl laughs, squirms, and contorts into these tiny giggles. This show is like a huge blast from my childhood.

Now that I'm here, on the couch, knowing I'm stuck, it's not so bad. Their little bodies are warm and soft. I actually like this a little. Maybe.

By the time the show's over, *I'm* ready for bed. I'm all cozy on the couch and warm.

"Time for bed." The little girl stands up and takes my hand.

Wait. "Don't kids hate to go to bed?"

"We share!" The little boy runs ahead and through a doorway, the little girl follows.

I stand in the door.

"Now you read us books."

"Me?" I ask. Which is a stupid thing to ask because of course *me*.

I sit and we read. More Dora. She's sort of numbing my brain after thirty minutes. No wonder Aidan's mom was teary when we came to watch her kids.

"Uh-oh…" the little girl says.

"Uh-oh, what?" I ask.

"My gum."

Gum? Are little kids allowed *gum*? I sit up off the bed and look around. Gum lying somewhere is not a good thing.

"Is there…" She points at me.

Oh. Great. On me. This is perfect. I look on the front of my shirt, and my shoulders, but I don't see anything.

Now they're both looking at me with their large blue eyes and smiling.

"Hair!" the boy says.

My stomach drops. Not in my hair. Please not in my hair. I run my hands down my head, and yep, about three inches up from the bottom is a knot of hair and gum. Great.

"Okay, you two." Now what? "Um…you can stay up as late

as you want, but if I hear anything, I come in and turn out the light, okay?"

They both grin.

Guess this is okay.

My heart's going all panicky as I step out of their room and feel my hair again. This is not good. I flick on the bathroom light, and yeah, it's even worse than I thought. I can't tell where my hair begins and the gum ends, it's all smashed in together.

And it's not like I have the best hair or anything, it's that…gum. *In my hair.*

Oh. Aidan. I flick off the bathroom light, head still spinning over the stupid hair situation. I take a few slow breaths before slowly turning the doorknob on the baby's room.

"'Bout time you showed up," Aidan whispers.

I stop. His hair is a little longer each time we get together, and I would have noticed sooner, but the whole babysitting thing sort of threw me. His blue eyes shine, even in the dark, and my stomach tightens at the way he's looking at me.

"Kate?" he asks because I've probably been staring at him too long.

"My hair." I pull the side forward to show him.

He tries to give me a sympathetic frown, but I can tell he's trying not to laugh. "Can you slide him in his bed?"

Oh. Right. Baby.

Now that I've leaned over, the warmth of him hits me, and we're close. Really close. Aidan's breath hits my face, and I slide my arms over his toned stomach and down his muscular arm to get my arms around the baby. And for the first time, I'm touching a guy who I'd really, really like to see with his shirt off. Our eyes catch, and his breath blows across my face. Whoa. Butterflies are running circuits through my insides, over a guy who's two years older, and only wants to hang with me so I can babysit with him.

What's wrong with me? I'm like all hormonal or something. Even making out with Shelton didn't make me all breathless like this. I scoop up the bundled baby, and lay him down in his bed, relieved I didn't break him or wake him or something.

I back away from the crib and run into the stomach and chest I was just thinking about.

"Sorry." My cheeks heat up and I stare at the floor, as if he'll somehow know what I'm thinking just by looking at him.

"Excuse me." He jumps back a step and holds the door for me to walk through.

Yeah. Guess it was awkward for both of us.

I go for the kitchen and sit at the table, trying to see the knotted mass in my hair.

"That is bad." He takes the chair next to me.

I let out a sigh as I realize the more I touch it, the worse it gets.

"Okay." His fingers touch the mass in my hair. "I have no idea what to do about this."

My chest sinks. "Well, I was thinking of cutting my hair anyway."

"Want me to cut it out for now?" he asks.

"Well, I definitely don't want to sleep on gum." Someone else's germs are in there. I shudder.

Aidan walks away, so I let myself notice him again while he can't watch me doing it. He's always in a plain white T-shirt. Always. It pulls across his chest and shoulders, just a little. But also, when he twists or turns a bit, I can see his sides, his abs, and his waist. The way I feel scares me. It's not the more-than-friends thing I felt with Shelton. It's more like want-my-hands-on-your-bare-skin and I can't believe I'm even *thinking* this. It's not like Shelton and I even went that far in our year together. Nothing under clothes. Ever. Okay, maybe a little on my back and waist, but that's it.

And here I am watching Aidan walk back toward me with a pair of scissors, and part of me wants to reach up under his shirt to feel his stomach.

I have problems.

"Can you do that with one arm?" I ask.

"Do you use two hands on scissors?" He widens his eyes a bit, and I can never tell if he's joking back, or if I've almost gone too far again.

"Uh...no. But I do use one hand to cut, and one to hold."

"Oh. Right." He stands to my left side and again, his breath hits my neck sending shivers through me. I'm pathetic. He's nineteen, waiting for disability, and I'm in high school. So not a good idea.

"I promise to be careful." He tries to hold in a laugh as he surveys the damage again.

"You know what?" I need to do something with all this pent-up energy. It's just hair, right? I can be bold. Forward. Cool. Unexpected. "Cut it all off, you know, all the way around."

"I can't." He shakes his head.

"It won't be pretty, but I can get that fixed later. I've always wanted shorter hair. My sister cuts hair. You know, I could do an a-line cut that's barely above my shoulders?"

"I don't even know what that is." He smirks.

"Just cut. Please. All the way around. Do it and get it over with." I squeeze my eyes tight.

I expect him to protest further, but he doesn't—just cuts and cuts. The sound of the scissors going through my hair is startling, crunching, smashing, something. It sounds like he's cutting through hair much thicker than mine, that's for sure.

"Done." He stands back. "It might be a little uneven in a spot or two." He tries to hold in his smile, which is my favorite thing because his cheeks get super dimpled.

I seriously need to stop thinking about him like this.

"I figured you'd put up some kind of protest." I slowly bring my hands to my head, and run them through my hair, top to bottom. The ends are a mangled mess, but my hair feels thicker, better.

"It's hair." He leans his face down to look up at me through his amazing lashes again. "Not an arm."

"Right. So since your perceptions are warped by your missing arm, my hair gets cut without a second thought?" I raise a brow.

He chuckles. "You wanted it. Besides, once someone evens the edges, it'll be perfect."

Great. Only I breathe in and smell some kind of lickable aftershave, and spearmint toothpaste—so, it was kind of worth it to have him so close.

"Come on. We have a few hours before they get back. Let's watch something."

And now I'm wondering how close I can sit next to him on the couch, but when we reach the living room I jump in the chair while he digs through movies. This is safer. Much, much safer.

8

AIDAN CONNELLY

Mom's hands come to her mouth as she and Stan step through the front door. "Kate, your hair," she gasps.

Kate's smile is wide. "I know. Your son did a terrible job. You know with only one arm and everything. I should have known."

"What?" Mom throws an accusing glare my way.

I start to defend myself when Kate speaks again. "There was an issue with gum, and it seemed like a good time to get it over with." Kate shrugs.

Mom's face falls. "Which one of the twins did it?"

Kate opens her mouth. "The...uh...girl?"

I chuckle because it's obvious she forgot her name, or never heard it to begin with.

"Well, let me pay to fix it at the very least." Mom starts rummaging in her purse.

"Mom. I got it," I say. "Kate thought we were going to hangout somewhere or something, and instead I dragged her here."

Mom stops. "Well thanks you two."

"Thank you," Stan adds.

"Oh!" Mom's face brightens. "My friend Janet owns a Regis, two blocks down. I know she's still there because her car was there when we came home."

"Isn't it kind of late?" I ask.

"My sister cuts hair. I'm good," Kate says. "Besides, what would I tell your friend Janet? Some one-armed guy attacked me with scissors?"

Mom's eyes widen slightly. I don't think she knows how to react. Kate has the great stunned look on her face that she always does when she blurts something like this out.

"No being sneaky around Kate." I toss my arm over her shoulder. "If you've got a missing limb, she'll notice every time."

Kate blushes and Mom chuckles as we step out the door.

I keep my arm around her for no real reason, just—she's here. But now that I'm thinking about it, maybe it's too much. Too personal. I jerk my arm away. No reason to keep her slim body close to me, even if it feels good.

"Thanks for coming with me," I say.

Her eyes find mine, but quickly look away, her cheeks turning pink. "It was interesting."

Interesting. It was that.

I lie in bed, once again unable to sleep.

I'm not good with girls. I wasn't the coolest guy in high school, and didn't have sex until I was in basic training. It's still amazing we found a way because we didn't get a whole lot of free time. When I was deployed, I was with an Air Force girl a few times. It was so casual. I'm lonely. You're lonely. Let's get together. Every time we camped in the Air Force camp, we'd get together. But a *girlfriend*? I don't even know where to start. I know I don't want the high school version of "going out." The whole smothering each other thing. But I also know I really want to spend time with her. With Kate.

I'm not sure how to balance it, and now the whole thing is sort of giving me a headache. I like her. The smell of her, the way she speaks, says things, smirks. And most of the time I think she doesn't like me, but tonight, the way she looked at me when I walked into the room with the scissors. There are a few things that make me feel like there might be something there.

But do I want there to be?

Kate swimming around in my head is keeping me awake just like the Army does. My forced departure from it. My friends still deployed in it. All of it. But thinking about Kate is better. For now. I think.

Foster takes me to lunch. We sit in a high-backed booth, and I could tell by the look on his face when he asked me here that it wasn't really an option thing. I mean, I guess it is, but no matter what, he'll find time to say what he wants to say. I might as well get a free burger. We order, and he starts to look a little nervous—shifting his weight back and forth.

"So, what's up?"

"I want to see how you're doing with everything."

"Everything, huh? That's kind of vague." I knew this was coming, but it sticks inside me just the same, making it hard to breathe.

"The list is long," he says. "I'm worried. I feel like I should be helping you in some way, but I don't know what to do."

The list is really long. My heart starts pounding in my ears and I can feel the words coming to the surface whether I want them to or not. "I hate my shrink. I've skipped physical therapy. I have nightmares, hate my calming drugs, and now I'm hanging out with Kate who I don't know what to do with. Mom's awesome and trying to help, but I don't know how she could with her new, crazy family, or even what to ask her. I'm supposed to be getting ready to go to college, or something, but it's hard to get motivated when I don't know what I want to do. My infantry unit comes back in weeks, and they all want me there, but I don't know if I can go. Pilot's wife needs to be visited, and I don't think I can do that either, or even if I want to. And then there's the matter of the car I love that I can't drive." I'm breathless at the end.

Foster scratches his head and taps his fingers on the table a few times.

"And this is why you always say fine and nothing when we ask you how you are and what we can do for you, right?" Foster leans over the table.

A lump stretches in my throat, and I nod. Unable to do more. It's so much. All of it is so much. Why the hell did we need to go somewhere public? I rest my elbow on the table and press my palm to my forehead. "Shit, I'm sorry," I whisper, as I try to get my body under control.

"Whoa, whoa. Don't be sorry." Foster reaches to the side, rubbing my shoulder a few times. "Aidan. Why don't you work on one thing, and then when you're feeling comfortable with that one thing, then work on something else."

"But it all needs to get done." I lift my head off my hand. "All of it."

"It does," he agrees. "But it doesn't all have to be done at the same time. You know what I mean?"

"I…I don't know."

"Let's tackle one thing at a time. First, Kate. You're spending time with a cool girl. Don't try and define it so much. If it's working, keep it working, if not, then don't. Just be straightforward with her. Honest. Because I really like Kate and neither of us wants to deal with the aftermath if Jen feels like you slighted her best friend." He chuckles. "Well, and Kate's almost another daughter around my house, so I might not be happy either."

"You're adding to the list of reasons it's not a good idea." I sit back in my seat.

Foster shakes his head. "That's not entirely what I meant."

"I'm. I'm going to try to push that one off a bit. Kate. Or maybe make things happen slow, or…I mean, I don't even know if she likes me, you know?"

His smile spreads a bit. "You like her."

"Can we hit on something else?" Anything to not be talking about girls with Foster would be good.

"Sure." Foster looks more relaxed already. Like we're planning a trip to Hawaii, and not my mess of a future. "It's pretty simple. Just sign up for school. You might not know what you want to do with your life until you get into school. One small step—maybe make an appointment with the guidance counselor at the community college. Your school is paid for. You need to take advantage of that. And I don't mind driving your car one bit, so no hurry there." He chuckles.

"Okay." One appointment. That I can do. And I can put off getting rid of my car.

"The therapy stuff, I can't help you with, Aidan. But Pilot's wife—"

"I might save that one for last." Way last. Or never. I might be okay with that too.

Foster just nods. "I've never…I mean, I can't even pretend to be able to understand that, Aidan. You know it's not your fault, and that—"

My whole gut seizes up. "No. It's the fucking bomb's fault, and whoever left it there." And he just happened to be standing on the right, instead of me. I pull in a few deep breaths through my nose as unclench the fists I didn't realize I'd tightened.

Foster shifts in his chair a few more times. Our waitress brings our burgers, but neither of us speaks.

There's so much. "And the guys. My guys. I know that's the other thing. It'll just…I don't know."

"Right now, worry about your guidance counselor appointment, okay? One thing."

One thing. And maybe I'll find a way to waste some time with Kate along the way.

"I'm glad you're staying with us, Aidan."

"Yeah, well…" I don't really have anywhere else to go. "It's not bad."

Foster laughs and for the first time actually relaxes in his seat. "I know it's not ideal for a nineteen-year-old guy looking to re-start his life, but—"

"It could be a hell of a lot worse."

"It could always be. Doesn't change what's happening now."

No. It doesn't. And as hard as it is to believe, it could all be worse. All of it. But it's not. I feel guilty as hell over it, but at least I have a future. A life to live, to enjoy. It's that I still have no idea what to do with it.

"Why do we do this on Saturdays again?" I wince as my therapist pushes my shoulder back as far as he can. He's this huge black guy, who has muscles that would make most people stand back a step, but talks feelings every time I'm here. Cracks me up.

"Because you, Aidan, said that you wanted to get a job and go to school and you couldn't have some *stupid therapy schedule mucking that up.*" His eyes widen as he messes with me.

"Right." I glance up at the TV—History Channel, just like he knows I like. I swear sometimes he's just sucking up. Fortunately, the small gym he calls his physical therapy office is pretty dead on Saturdays.

Bradley releases my shoulder, and I see spots the thing hurts so bad.

"Do you get some sort of thrill out of hurting people like this?" I ask.

He ignores my comment, like always. "Seeing anyone?"

"Um…I don't know." I scrunch my face up as he pushes forward.

"You don't know?" He chuckles. "Relax, Aidan. I'm just trying to keep you stretched out."

"We've gone out a few times." *Seeing* someone feels serious. Like tied in or something. And it's not that I guess I mind, but it feels forward, final, uncomfortable…"Not really *out*, out." I helped her make her boyfriend jealous, ditch school, and she helped me babysit. Suddenly it all seems a bit juvenile.

"Kissed her yet?" He wags his brows.

"Dude are you my shrink or are you here to make sure my shoulder doesn't completely seize up?" I snap. I don't want to talk about Kate. I don't want to be in physical therapy. My first thing was to talk to a guidance counselor, but the exhaustion of dealing with all the other crap is fucking, not mucking, it all up.

"Whoa, Aidan. Just making small talk." Bradley sits back and forces us to make eye contact. Like we're all good pals because he's helping me learn how to live with one arm.

"Right." I can't small talk with anyone. Nothing in my life is small. It's all huge things—huge decisions, huge consequences.

"Touchy subject then." He folds his arms signaling the end of my torture.

"No," I snap again.

"Okay." But his brows go up, which makes me not believe him, and I suddenly want to call Kate because I need to just hang out. Get away from this list I'm supposed to be doing, because doing things one at a time isn't going so well for me.

9

Kate Walker

It's the first real smile I've seen on my sister since arriving.

"You're really going to let me cut your hair?" My sister lives to cut hair. Do makeup. Have pretty nails…

"Well you can't do any worse than Aidan did." I shrug. "It's a mess, and I'd rather not look like a freak, even though it's Saturday. Also, it does look bad enough that people will believe me when I say it was cut by a one-armed man." I'm all pleased with myself for making a joke, but it's Aidan, and he's not here, so maybe I shouldn't have.

"Who's Aidan?" Deena's brows come together, and she takes another small bite of dry granola. Gross.

"Jen's cousin." I start to say he picked me up when I skipped school the other day, but Mom and Dad are in the kitchen. "He lost his arm in Afghanistan."

"Oh…" Her voice falls into that sickeningly sweet, sad, pity voice that I'm sure he hates as much as I do. "He's so *young*."

"Nineteen, and pretty awesome to hang out with." I pull a chair to sit in front of my sister, scissors in hand.

Now she has that really annoying look on her face that says she knows something I don't. "You *like* him. Are you two going out or something?"

I spin away from her and sit on the chair as I feel my cheeks heat up. "No. I helped him babysit his little brothers and sister, that's all."

Her fingers start running through my hair—surveying the damage. "And how was that?"

All I can see is Aidan's snug T-shirt as he walked toward me with his oh-so-perfect smile. "Good." I clear my throat, trying to recover.

Deena leans slightly. "Uh...huh..." She's wearing that really annoying smile again. The one that means *I see what's going on, and you'll never convince me different.*

Yeah, didn't fool her any. And this means that maybe I do *like* him, like him. How crazy is that?

Deena's scissors start lightly snipping through my hair, so I concentrate on holding still. No need for me to make it even shorter than it already is.

"Look. Even if I did like him, it doesn't matter. Aidan's probably going through a lot. He's like, an adult."

"You're nearly eighteen, Kate. And your life this past year hasn't exactly been peachy." She leans forward to look me in the eye. Her face turns an odd shade of pale green. "Okay, no leaning." She takes a few deep breaths as she slowly rises back to standing.

"Please don't puke on my hair, okay?" I try to make it sound light, but the thought of it makes me cringe.

She chuckles once. "We're not changing the subject. I think you two have more in common than you think you do, and I can tell when my sister likes someone. Also, he lost an arm in something that was probably a lot more tragic than your pass-out and trip to the hospital, but both of you are dealing with new things that'll affect you forever."

Forever.

There's that stupid word again. I don't want forever. The thought of carrying my finger pricker and my shots around for another year make me want to scream, but forever? That stuns me into silence.

Deena rambles on about how big the baby is now and names that her and Lane are thinking of. I sit and stare at the wall as my hair drops to the floor.

My least favorite thing: Sitting in the waiting room at the doctor's office. With Dad. Sucks. I'll endure the same questions, and the same warnings I always do.

Okay, well. It would be worse if Mom was here too because she always gets this weird worried-frowny look on her face that kills me.

I run my hands over my smooth, shiny hair. Why didn't it look this thick and healthy when it was six inches longer? Seems completely unfair. I catch my reflection in a mirror on the far side of the room and smile. Like a dork. Even my cheekbones look better with my hair this way.

Who would have thought so much good could come from a wadded up mass of hair, gum, and little-kid sticky fingers?

The nurse calls me back and we do the routine. Dad's waits in the exam room. The endocrinologist (my diabetes doctor) is a friend of his. Of course.

Weight. Check.

Height. Check.

Do they think I might change that much in two months? Are they worried I might start shrinking?

Blood sugar even though I showed her the one I did a couple hours ago. Check.

Frowny face on the nurse. Check.

Pee in a cup. Make a ridiculous mess. Try not to think about pee on my hands as I scrub. Check.

Now time to wait for my doctor. Dr. Masen. With my dad. In silence.

So, my doc isn't a bad guy as doctors go. But I shouldn't need to be in here at all, or maybe it's more that I don't want to be.

"Kate, how are we this morning?" He's older than my dad with white hair, but has more energy.

"Fine." I did a great job of making my voice sound all relaxed and good, so that's nice, but I remember today is one of four visits a year where they have the results of my cellular level screening test, and Mom forgot with the excitement of Deena around. So one thing's working in my favor today.

"Fine." He looks through the notes on his computer, his face turning sterner and his eyes narrowing.

"Can I see your book?" He holds out his hand, frowning.

I slowly pull it from my purse and give it to him. The one Mom bought for me. The one she thought would make it more fun because it's pink, sparkly, and looks like it belongs in an eight-year-old's Barbie room. He won't like how up and down my blood sugar has been. It's sometimes hard after school and stuff. Well, and it's hard in the morning, even though Mom tries.

"Are you honest when you write down your levels?" He turns a page, and his eyes don't meet mine.

I open my mouth to answer, but close it again. Dad's eyes are practically drilling holes into my brain right now, but I keep my eyes on Doc. Safer.

He sighs and hands me my book. "Your book does me no good if you're not putting the actual numbers in there."

Once again I open my mouth to protest, but I really have nothing that'll change the crappiness of this situation.

"I got your HbA1C test back. Any guess on where you're at?" he asks as he leans back.

Dad's not doing any of his specialized breaths. Maybe he's not breathing at all.

"The cellular level test right?" I ask, even though I know that's exactly what he's talking about. I also know where I should be, and where I'm probably not.

He nods once. "A normal, non-diabetic person would be at about a four point eight, and six point five would be someone I'd consider as being on the edge of out of control with their levels. Care to guess where you fall?"

My heart starts pounding. "Um...six point five?" And a small smile starts to creep in.

He frowns further. "A twelve, Kate. A twelve."

Dad pushes out a breath. It's his hurt-angry-exhausted one. He even rubs his hand over his thinning hair several times as the room sits in gelled silence.

"Um..." But I have nothing to say. Nothing to add.

"No reaction from you at all?" Doc's brows go up.

"I..." How bad can that be? "Didn't you tell me that you have patients who go between ten and twelve?"

The moment the words leave my lips, I know it's not the right thing to say.

"Yes. I do." He goes stoic. "They die much younger than my patients who keep theirs under control. You are very lucky right now in that you're young, and if you work at it, you could easily be under that six point five mark."

I hear Dad sniff and I look over to see his hand over his mouth and him blinking back tears. There's so many millions of tiny pinpricks in my chest that there's no way to keep his sadness out. Now *I'm* blinking back tears.

This is the whole way-too-real stuff I wanted to disappear with the hospital.

Die. Early.

The words stab hard into me bringing all the scared stuff to the surface that I try to keep pushed away.

"I'm going to recommend an insulin pump again." His eyes go from me to Dad.

I clutch my stomach afraid I'll throw up, and shake my head. "Please no. Please, please. I can't have that." I can't have something practically permanently attached to me, IN me. No way. I know it's just a tiny little box—some little tiny thing stuck in me, but *it's a little tiny thing stuck in me*. All the time.

No. Way.

"Kate, please." Dad turns toward me and it's completely unfair because he just looks so…*sad*.

"One more chance. I'll do anything." My breath's coming more quickly and my eyes go from Dad to doc to Dad. "Please."

"Jeremy." The doctor looks at Dad, and I know he wants him to talk me into it. This is the really, really sucky part about them being friends—on a first-name basis even.

They lock eyes for a moment and then Dad slumps.

"Last chance, sweetie. But no more fudging, and you're going to have to text or call each and every time you check levels and give yourself a shot. No late nights. No sleepovers." Dad seems almost sad about the restrictions, but it doesn't change the suckiness of the situation.

"So, if I don't want some needle stuck in me twenty-four/seven, I'm *grounded?*" That's exactly what it's sounding like to me.

"Kate." Doc snaps. His harsh voice silences me. "I'm about to put my nose where it doesn't belong. Look at your dad."

He pauses until I do. Dad's face is etched with worry. It's around his eyes and in the way the corners of his mouth are pulled down. Guilt tugs at me, and I hate it.

"He's scared to death that you're going to kill yourself, or do some serious permanent damage because you don't care enough to be careful here. Don't turn this around on him."

I nod. "Fine. But no stuck-in-me-all-the-time needles. Please."

"They're not needles, they're—"

I hold my hand up. "I know. Doesn't matter."

He sighs. "This disease isn't horrible to live with if you just…"

But I'm tuned out. *Disease.* All I picture when I hear that word is rotting bodies, lepers or something. Something eating, chewing away at me. I shudder.

"Kate?"

"I'm sorry, what?"

He sighs again, probably knowing that I wasn't paying attention.

"Online groups? Kids your age dealing with the same thing?"

"Oh…uh…not yet." What will they be able to tell me that I don't already know?

We sit in silence, staring, almost like a challenge. Who will speak first?

"This isn't going to go away simply because you want it to," Doc says.

It might.

"I know you're dealing with a lot. A whole new schedule of eating and testing, but it'll get easier. I promise you there will come a day when you hardly think about it."

Yeah. Right.

"I'd really like to see you connecting with people your own age who are dealing with all the same things."

Not likely.

"I don't like how much you're allowing your levels to bounce around. I'm going to be calling your house to make sure that both you and your parents are monitoring you as closely as they need to." Doc's eyes go between us again.

I can feel the really stupid thought coming out of my mouth, and I try to hold it in, but it comes just the same. "They're already being strict after the whole car thing."

"Because we all thought that would help snap you back to the reality where this is a *really big deal!*" Dad shouts.

I jump in my chair, and then stare at my feet. "Lecture point made. I'll be more careful." Can this meeting *please* be over?

"I'm not convinced. Do we need to go over what can happen to you if your body goes into a diabetic coma? Not everyone comes out of those." Doc's voice is softer now.

If I could cover my ears and scream la-la-la-la-la I totally would. But I can't. I'd really piss him off if I did that. Well, and he'd probably call Mom. I'm lucky she's not in here with me right now because if Dad's close to tears, Mom would definitely be crying.

I'm shaking, but trying really hard not to show it.

"Please do what we've asked you to do, Kate. It might seem like a lot, but I promise it'll help."

"Thanks. We done for today?" I ask. Because I really need out.

"We're done."

Thank God. "Thank you."

Dad rests his arm over me, but I still feel like I'm swimming from information overload that I'm wishing to forget. The moment we leave the building he pulls me into a tight hug. "If I could take this from you, I would, Katie. I'm so sorry."

Dad almost breaks down the final walls. I know because I can feel tears threatening my eyes again, and I don't want to think about this. It's too much. Too real. Too much forever stuff that I can't imagine having to deal with. And it's so much easier when he's mad at me than when he starts to wish as much as I do that it would go away.

"I'm hungry. Can we go home?" I ask. Anything to avoid Dad's sorrow.

Dad let out a breath—a sad one. "Yes, Katie. We can go home."

Mom's in tears after she and Dad talk. She's berating herself over and over for not being there, for not missing Deena's appointment in favor of mine. For not looking at her calendar more closely. And the moment they know I'm near, it goes silent, but both their eyes are on me. I'm really going to have to be careful.

"AJ's yearly birthday bash is this weekend. You going?" Jen slides her arm through mine as we head up the hallway.

"I don't know." I make a face. "With all my new restrictions, it might be hard."

"Your parents trust me. I'll ask them." She grins.

"That'd actually be great." Anything to give me some space would be great.

"I bet Aidan would go…" She wiggles her brows.

My heart jumps, and I want to grab both her shoulders and ask, *Do you really think so?*

But I don't. We keep walking. "Yeah…maybe I'll ask him."

"*Maybe* you will." She smirks and gives me a sideways shove into US Government.

And the second I think I can get away with it, meaning Mr. Decker's behind his computer, I pull out my phone because sending a text to Aidan about getting together is way better than texting my parents the latest insulin shots and blood sugar numbers.

Stupid hs party this wknd. Wanna go? Your cousins will be there.

And hit Send.

I get a message a moment later. *I could be talked into it.*

Now I hope that he wants to be talked into it in person, because I sort of want an excuse to see him again. For him to see my new hair and improved cheekbones. And maybe to distract me from the weight that's been pushing on my chest since the doctor's appointment.

I stuff my phone back into my pocket, biting my lip to hold in the beginnings of a ridiculous grin, and Shelton's watching me.

Watching me in a way that makes my heart jump. The problem is that I don't know if that's good anymore because I'm definitely distracted by someone else. And God knows I'm in desperate need of distraction right now so I look back to my desk. Where it's safe. For now.

10

AIDAN CONNELLY

"I thought you were picking me up." Kate smirks as she steps out of Jen's car. She's wearing a short jacket that stops right at the smallest part of her waist where I'm now staring.

Jen waves, and pulls out to get Toby. "See you there!"

Kate tosses her hair out of her eyes, and I can't stop staring, her face went from pretty to beautiful with shorter hair. Her black T-shirt is cut lower than normal, showing the hint of the curve of her chest. My heart starts pounding because even though we've been alone before, this is the first time we've been alone where it *feels* alone. Like there's possibility. Like I might want to touch her.

"She said your parents were upset about something and would only let you leave with her." That's the story I got anyway. Now I'm wondering if it's something different.

"Oh. Right." Kate frowns and pulls her huge bag/purse thing up higher on her shoulder.

"I haven't figured out how to drive my car," I say. Needing to distract myself from staring.

"Oh." Her brows come together making her look confused.

I toss her my keys as I step toward the passenger's side. The top's already down, ready for our night.

She climbs in, hoists her bag between the seats and looks across the dash. "This car is amazing."

"Had it forever," I say.

And she is looking at it the way I hoped she would—like she's impressed.

I sit back in the passenger's seat and close the door. It's actually nice being in the passenger's seat because my missing arm is less noticeable from here. Not that either of us forgets; it's just nice when it's not completely out there. I look normal from her side anyway.

"I don't get the big deal," she says as she buckles in. "You've driven me before, and I'm always driving with one hand. I'm drinking a soda, eating a sandwich, texting…"

"You can't text and drive." I can't take my eyes off of her. She's pretty, funny, wants to be here with me, and it's still sort of surprising.

"You can if you have two hands instead of one." She gives me another smile, but her face sort of freezes like it does when she's worried she's gone too far.

"That was low." I lean toward her, and my hand twitches thinking about touching her hair, or her tiny chin. I'm pathetic, and probably shouldn't have accepted her invitation. At the same time I'm glad that Jen took her brother so Kate and I are alone.

She shakes her head. "Sorry. It's like I'm missing that filter of—*hey, this is something you shouldn't say.*"

"It's cool. At least I'll know where I stand with you." I definitely need that.

"Yes. You probably will." Only her face changes making me think she's thinking something else.

She puts the key in the ignition and takes a quick look down. "I don't know how to drive a stick."

Perfect. "So, even with your two arms, you can't drive a standard? I thought you could text and drive," I tease.

"I can, but this…I mean, I'll ruin your car. I don't know what to do." Her eyes are wide as she shakes her head. "I really should have put that together. I mean, it didn't make any sense that you could drive your uncle's car and not this one."

"You're smart. You can figure it out." I taught Will. Surely I can teach her too. It's not the same as driving it myself, but I put an ad on Craigslist, and I want to take another drive in my car before it's gone.

"I…What do I do?"

I start to explain about shifting, and the clutch and the gas when she gets out of the car.

"What?" I crack my door as she comes around to my side. The other cars are gone. I don't want our night ruined, just because she's afraid to drive my car. This is the kind of ridiculous girl thing I didn't want to deal with.

"You're driving. I'm not doing it." Her eyes don't find mine and she doesn't slow as she comes to the passenger's side door.

My frustration over not being able to drive my car turns to anger. "I can't drive the damn thing!" I push to standing already breathing hard. "I've tried! The stick and the steering wheel are too far apart! I can't even make a turn!"

She puts a hand on my chest, almost like she's going to push me away. Not bothered at all by my yelling. "I'll shift. You do the whole clutch, gas, steer thing."

I open my mouth to argue, but I suddenly feel pretty dumb for not thinking about it earlier. And I'm completely distracted by how her hand feels on my chest. As her hand slides down, her eyes follow, and I want for her to have wanted to touch me way more than I should.

All I hear is my breathing and I'm still staring at her hand, which is now nearly to the top of my jeans.

She drops her arm, and steps around me leaving me feeling very on edge, and maybe a bit like I want her to touch me that way again. I go around the front of the car and climb into the driver's seat—still feeling the heat from her touch. I have no idea if I'm thrilled or terrified that I said yes to going with her tonight. Kate isn't like Georgia, my Air Force girl. It wouldn't be a hook-up once in a while kind of thing. Nerves start to press in.

I settle into the seat, and the car takes over my thoughts. I love this car. I run my hand over the top of the steering wheel a few times.

"When you're done fondling your vehicle, I need you to show me how to shift."

I chuckle, and turn as sideways as I can, pushing the clutch in with my left foot.

"Put your hand on the shift."

She does. Her hair falls over her face a bit as she looks down, but I can still make out her dark eyes staring in concentration.

"Now you just follow the map on the top, you'll feel a bump and then you're in neutral, pull it back farther and you'll be in second."

She pulls down and the shifter goes slack in neutral.

"Now what?" Her eyes are still focused on her hand.

"Pull back more and you'll slide into second."

She concentrates for a few moments, and jerks, but nothing happens. I scoot even farther sideways to put my left hand over hers. Our eyes catch. Okay. Breathe. This is just a girl. No big deal.

"Okay, first." I move our hands into first. "Second." I move our hands again. We go through all the gears a few times. My hand on hers. Me trying to keep my heart beating normal, trying to force my chest to relax. This is crazy. I'm just touching her hand.

"You ready?" I take mine back. Kate is not a good idea. At all. Nothing that makes me feel this much is a good idea.

"Sure."

I push in the clutch and start the car. This engine doesn't purr, it growls. I'm really going to miss this car. "Okay reverse…*now*," I say as I push in the clutch.

Kate's got it. Easy.

We back onto the roadway. "First...*now*."

Again she has it perfect, and she smiles wide as the car moves forward.

I hit the gas, hard, then clutch. "Second, *now*."

And we're flying.

Every time I let myself look over at her, shiny, short hair blowing in the wind, her grin fills her face. She's loving this almost as much as I am. We're weaving up through a canyon now, heading to a high school party I let myself get talked into. But I don't care where we're going because I'm in my car, which means I'm already right where I want to be.

We're doing about seventy-five, and I'm loving every second of it.

"Get ready to shift down," I say.

"But you're going too fast."

"Third, *now*." I stuff my foot onto the clutch and she does as I asked. The car screeches around the corner.

Kate screams, but it's followed by a laugh, and I realize she's driving with a one-armed guy, through a narrow canyon, shifting without question. Not only is she a pretty cool girl, she also trusts me—I don't know if I've ever had that with a girl before.

"It's up here." She points only briefly and then both her hands go back to the stick. "See the lights?"

And I can't really miss it. The house has yard lights that glow off the hillside and trail down to the road. Kate shifts down for me a few times as I direct, completely unquestioning as we pull up the huge parking lot/driveway with a view of the river below.

The house looks like a massive log cabin. Massive. Two stories or more. Huge windows. Enormous logs.

"You're here!" Jen waves, her eyes on me instead of on Kate. "Will's puking his guts out in the backyard. Can you go check on him?"

My stomach sinks. I don't want to play babysitter to my cousin. Not tonight.

Kate's eyes find mine, but I swear something's different. She's looking at me different, really taking me in. The same way I've been taking her in since she showed up tonight.

"I'll meet you inside. He's your cousin, so you have that whole family obligation thing going on." She winks, climbs out, and follows Jen in through the basement door.

Now I get to go find Will, although I have no idea how he got to puking drunk that fast.

I wander around the side of the large house, and see Will stumbling toward a small bench.

"You're a pathetic specimen, man," I tease as Will finally gets to sitting.

"I know," he croaks. "It was the final two shots. They hit my stomach hard." Will's the perfect example of why I've never been much of a drinker. Probably he normally isn't either—making his problems tonight even worse.

I half prop him up, his arm wrapped around a decorative rock, which he's now clutching like his life depends on it. I sit and lean back on the bench in front of the log cabin/mansion and take in the view. The winding river is incredible from here. I can see miles down the canyon. Will's breathing has steadied a bit, so I'm thinking he might be past the puking. Now I feel kind of bad because I came with Kate, and I've been sitting outside with my cousin for probably close to an hour.

But it shouldn't matter. It's not like we're *together*, together. She's just cool. Like making it so I could drive my own car. The porch is pretty full, but I scan the faces anyway. And there's Kate. Wide, brown eyes right on me. It hits me hard, leaving an aftershock of tingling.

No one in my position should even be thinking about being with a girl. Not the way I'm thinking about her. The way that makes me want to have the warmth of her pressed against me, her lips on mine, and her mouth on my neck.

Okay. Deep breaths. I shouldn't be doing this right now.

She gives me a small wave, and I stare. Like a moron. She spins around and walks back inside.

"You okay?" I ask Will, suddenly desperate to know what Kate's thinking.

"Okay," he whispers, readjusting his grip on the rock. "Jen and Toby are giving me a ride home. I'm good. I'm just going to stay out here…where it's cool."

Right. Good. I jog to the downstairs door and go inside. If I thought the music was loud from the backyard, it's nothing compared to how it is now. Not even good music either, some hip-hop or pop or whatever. Not my thing. I scan for Kate and try not to notice if or how anyone's looking at me. I side step around a pool table that's hovered around by a pretty big group. Pool is another thing I can't do anymore. Or, at least I haven't figured out how to yet. When I hit the top of the stairs, she's not up here either.

"Where's Shelton?" Toby asks someone in the kitchen.

Right. The other reason I need to leave Kate alone.

Whoever's standing in front of the fridge laughs. "He and Tamara went in search of a room..."

Okay then. Maybe that's why Kate's not around. Half of me feels bad for her and the other half wants to scream that she could do so much better.

What, like you?

I don't even want to be involved with anyone, I tell myself.

Not even Kate?

Especially not Kate. I like her too much to bring her into my mess.

"Did you come here with Kate?" Shelton folds his arms over his chest trying to look tougher than he is I'd guess.

"Yeah." But how do I play this? I mean, I like Kate, but I'm pretty sure she still likes him. "I'm Jen's cousin."

His eyes float to where my arm should be—everyone's do—and

he continues to look at me. "Are you two…" he trails off, hoping maybe that I'll pick up and answer his question without him having to ask.

"Am I correct in that *you* dumped *her*?" I smile a little, hoping that'll diffuse some of the tension in my voice.

"Well—"

"And a guy would have to be a moron not to like Kate." I figure this shows where I stand without giving too much away.

"Shelton?" A too-skinny blond comes around the corner in the hallway.

"Gotta run. Nice meeting you." And then I spin around purposefully leaving out my name. This way he'll have to ask her about me if he wants to know. Or maybe he'll be sneaky and ask Jen. And *this* is why I should not be involved with a high school girl. I've already stooped to playing games.

After spending another ten minutes or so wandering the house of obnoxious people, and no luck finding Kate, I decide to get some air.

The second I hit the driveway I see the top of her head, in the backseat of my car, staring at the sky. I stand and watch her for a minute. Easily prettier than any girl I've ever been with. She comes from this smart, good family. I still don't know how to be with a girl only having one arm—and maybe she's more bothered by my loss of an arm than she seems to be. Maybe she really thinks of us as just friends, so this worrying is for nothing.

Okay, Aidan. This is where you go back inside, and pretend you didn't see her out here.

But I'm walking toward her anyway—like I'm being pulled. I climb in and sit next to her in the backseat.

"Hey," she says, letting her wide eyes find mine.

"Hey." I slide down until our faces are level—both of us slouched.

"I just...I don't know. It's loud, and I know those people. I mean, they're my friends, but..."

I want to ask her about Shelton. Really want to ask her. But it might fall under things you just don't ask people. Though she asks me that stuff all the time.

"Are you out here because of Shelton?"

She giggles. "No. I mean, I don't know. At this point I'm more disappointed in him than anything else. And did you see what he was wearing? It's like he was headed to some political rally or something filled with over-achieving college students, not AJ's yearly birthday party."

"Yeah." I slide lower and now our faces are close. Way too close. *Not a good idea. Not a good idea.* My eyes float down her face. Down her high cheekbones, pink lips. And I want her closer, but I don't get Kate. Shouldn't want Kate. We're both in a weird place right now. Me because I lost my career and her...well, she just lost her boyfriend. Maybe none of it is worth worrying about.

She lets out a little sigh that sounds more like contentment than anything else.

I stop thinking and lean toward her until our lips are together. It's been too long. Way too long. Her lips are warm and soft, and all it does is make me want more. Crave it.

She kisses me back, opening her mouth, deepening our kiss. I'm shocked she does it, but it feels good to feel wanted like this. Way better than I was thinking.

"Wow," she whispers. "I wanted to kiss you."

I chuckle, because what else am I supposed to do when a girl says something like that. "Well, *that's* good." I think. Maybe I should have wished for her to not want to kiss me. Maybe this is going to be too much. Maybe she'll expect something from me that I have no idea how to do. Maybe I'm just really, really over-thinking this pretty ideal situation of being in the backseat of my car with a hot girl.

"You know what I mean." She adjusts herself so the side of her face is resting on the back of the seat next to me. Staring at me with her deep, brown eyes.

"Uh...no. I don't know what you mean."

"Just that, we hang out. You know?"

"Yeah. I know. I'm there, when we *hang out*," I tease.

"Never mind." She puts her hand on my chest and stares at it for a moment, before resting it on my neck, pulling us together. "Kiss me again."

"No." I turn my head, teasing. "I want to know what you mean first."

"Just that you're you, and all moody, and nothing like the kind of guy I thought I'd be with, but I want this. You. I mean, I want to be here." Her fingers tracing my neck and shoulder are killing me in such a good way. It's crazy what this girl is doing to me, especially since I was really trying to not feel what I'm feeling right now.

Moody. Yeah, I guess. "You thought you'd end up with someone like Shelton."

"Yeah." She kisses the corner of my mouth. "But this is better."

"How much better?" My lips touch hers as I speak.

"Better enough that I want your hand on me."

I don't even have to look to know her cheeks are turning red, and that she probably just said something she didn't mean to. This is when her bursts of honesty are really going to help. She leans forward until the top of her head is pressed into my chest, hiding. Her arms wrap around my sides, keeping us together.

"I can't believe you just said that." I kiss her softly on the temple, and run my hand slowly up and down her arm.

"Me either."

I touch her chin until she lifts her head from my chest and looks back up at me. It's stupid, but I want her to kiss me first this time. Like I want to make sure she really does want this as much as I do.

But now I wonder—what will she actually think about me only having one arm? What will happen when she accidentally runs her hand over where my arm should be? Will it matter? Will she care?

I'm actually relieved that my shoulder stump is against the seat. Out of reach.

She leans forward and our lips come together in a small soft kiss, before pulling away. I kiss her back, but this time our kiss is deep enough that the electricity flies through my body sending tingles to my toes, fingertips, every piece, every part. All of it. And I should probably be thinking more, but it feels so good to not think, to just feel. I slide my arm around her waist, frustrated I don't have more power to keep her close, and kiss her again.

11

Kate Walker

I never thought I could wake up the morning after kissing a boy, and still feel it. But wow, *two days later* and I still feel it. I feel it while I'm getting ready for school, and as I rest my chin on my hands in class. Each time a finger taps my lips, I close my eyes and remember Aidan's fingers touching my lips just before his mouth did.

I'm smart enough to know this isn't a safe thing to think about at school, especially with my lack of speaking filter or whatever, but I can't take my mind off him. His mouth. His body. His cocky smile—the one that doesn't come out as often as I want it to.

And even with my practical (and really embarrassing) invitation to put his hand all over me. He didn't. Okay, he kind of did. But not really, not even as much as I wanted him to. And that's a first.

He's the perfect distraction from everything that's wrong in my life right now, which I love almost as much as the kissing.

"What's with you?" Jennifer asks as we step out of English.

"What do you mean?"

"Uh…the obvious fact that you haven't mentioned Shelton or

stared at him all day and that you're staring into space, and that we were talking Faulkner in AP English and you didn't offer *anything*."

This is sort of big here. Because Jen set us up, but I don't think she believed it would actually go anywhere, and that changes things a bit. But if *he* tells her, and I don't say anything, she'll be mad. I mean, she should be mad because I'm her best friend and I didn't say, "I kissed your cousin." Crap. There it is. My honest mouth.

"What?" She grabs my arm, her eyes wide. I don't know this face. This face is a new one. Is it good? Bad? Does the know? Crappity, crap, crap.

"We, um, kissed. Saturday night. At the party. Well, actually in his car in the driveway at the...party..." I'm staring, concentrating, hoping to decipher the look on her face.

"Okay. I thought this would be cool. But this is weird. I mean, you guys aren't really suited for each other, you know?" She lets my arm go and grabs her books with two hands.

I open my mouth to protest, but I really can't. She's right. We're not. Not in a conventional way. "I know."

"Do you like him?"

I squeeze and push, and try to keep my smile from spreading, but I can't.

"You really like him." Her eyes are wide, and there's a slight smile, but she still looks confused.

"It's different. Like he's older, and he gets me, and doesn't care that I say stupid things, at bad times. And..."

"Okay, well. Cool, I guess."

"I mean, I don't even know what we are right now, but it's good." I'm holding my breath waiting for her response.

"Honestly. It's weird, but okay."

"Okay." I lean against my locker feeling a little light-headed.

"I'm off." She makes a face. "Mr. A's a real prick when we're late."

"See ya." Only as the hallways continue to empty out, I'm still leaning against my locker waiting for my body to stop feeling like I'm on a boat instead of solid ground. This is stupid. I need to get to class.

The hallways are empty, and my eyesight is a little blurry as I walk to class suddenly feeling way on edge. My heart is racing, and frustration courses through me. Did I do my shot at lunch? Spots. Spots. My bag's in my locker. An apple. A piece of ham. I *should* be okay, but when was my last shot? Oh. I stole some of Jen's roll. That could be it. Mom'll be pissed. I wonder how high my levels are. I'm going to get another lecture about how I should count and shoot up before I eat instead of after.

No-no-no-no-no.

I've been doing so well after my doctor's appointment. This is not good. I lean against the doorway of my classroom but don't go in. I blink a few more times and turn back to my locker.

"Kate?" Shelton's voice calls out behind me. "You need help?"

He's even better than Mom at recognizing the signs of my highs and lows.

"I'm good." I wave him off. And he's sort of the last place I want help from anyway. "And I definitely don't need help from *you.*"

He jogs up and rests his hand on my arm, but I don't slow. "Don't be like that, Kate. We should be friends."

I'm so stupid. I'm supposed to be managing better. Dad's going to be so upset.

His hands feel so familiar. His dark skin against mine. "You forgot to do your shot, didn't you?"

I let out a huff. I'm just so irritated. Why does he have to know me so well?

"You always get all agitated when your level gets high." His voice is so annoying, normal and calm.

"I don't get agitated unless someone's agitating me." I stop at my locker and start working the combination only my fingers feel funny and the numbers aren't coming to me.

"Kate?" He tries to catch my eyes by leaning down.

I stop working, and look at him.

"Let's get you to the nurse."

My frustration dissolves just that fast.

He knows what I need. Shelton was there the day I passed out. He was there when we went through all the testing. We hadn't even been going out all that long, and he was there. He stayed with me through all of that, and now that I've been at my new normal for a while, that's when he decided to bail? And why would I care when I've been thinking about Aidan and his lips all day?

Shelton's familiar arm is around me, and I lean into him. Not as much because I like him, but because my world's swimming right now, and I need to remember what I ate, and know what my blood sugar is so I know how much insulin to take.

Why didn't I do this right at lunch when I'm supposed to? It would have been so much easier. Now there's another thing Shelton can add to the list he probably keeps of why Kate is crazy.

"You should have done this during lunch hour, Kate."

I really hate it when people point out the obvious—especially when I've already figured it out.

"Okay, almost there. You're quiet, which kind of scares me." His voice is the same warm, soft voice that used to tell me he loved me. Talked to me until I couldn't keep my eyes open. Read my homework to me while I spent a few days in the hospital getting adjusted to my new life.

"I'm okay. Sorry, and thank you." Because at least I'm smart enough to know that being as petty as I'd like to be right now won't earn me anything.

He keeps his arm firmly on my side and pulls open the nurse's door, leading me to one of the horrible vinyl beds.

"So you mind?" He goes to the high cupboard that's supposed to be locked, but never is. My stuff's in there. Shelton knows this. He knows so much. *Did* we turn into friends?

Guess it doesn't matter because we're not together, and he

did not handle our breakup well. Okay, so neither did I. But still. Neither did he.

Shelton pulls a hard, plastic chair up to the bed.

I sit back and lean against the cool wall.

He hands me my small tester. I stick my finger in and wait for the prick.

"Kate!" Shelley rushes to my side. And yes, I'm on a first name basis with the school nurse. Just another perk.

"She'll be okay." Shelton chuckles. "I've seen her a lot worse. She's only a little high." He checks my reader. "Or *way* high. You're above three hundred, Kate."

I cringe. Mom's going to be pissed. My lows come on a lot faster and feel a lot worse, but I guess it's the highs that do real damage. I don't like to think about that much, so I don't.

Shelley clutches her hands together, and looks at me with her teeny little frowny face.

"Want me to do your shot?" Shelton asks.

I'm an idiot. I nod. I hate doing it, and Shelton was always the best. Better than Mom, better than Dad. It's like he could take me out of the equation.

"Thank you." I lie down. My ex-boyfriend is about to pull a pinch of fat from my stomach to give me my shot. This is just... well there aren't words.

"Let's find the fattiest part of Kate," he teases.

His fingers slide a few inches to the right of my belly button, he pulls on my skin, pinching as big an area as he can. And yes, having a guy know how to pinch my fat is definitely humiliating, but we've done it for so long...

"Ow." I scrunch my eyebrows down as I feel the prick. Anyway, he's better at it than I am—probably 'cause it's not his own skin he's pushing into.

"Oh, whatever." He chuckles as he pulls my shirt down. "You know I did better than you would've."

"Thanks." It's so weird being this close to him again. Part of me feels like we were never apart. But we were apart. *Are* apart.

Then Tamara's face appears in my mind, grasping his arm, and grinning up at him like a love-struck freshman.

"What's that face?" he asks.

"Tamara."

He sighs. "I really don't want to have this conversation."

"It's fine. Thanks for helping me out." Even though I hate asking for help, and hate getting it. Mostly, I hate needing it.

"Kate." He takes my hand and I close my eyes. Determined not to look at him. "I don't want you to think that I don't care about you, but it changed. More like friends. And I want that, okay? Us to be friends. We were close for a long time, and it would be a waste to lose that."

He has such a condescending *adult* voice. "Whatever, Shelton. You'd better get to class."

He pushes out a sigh. Like my dad. A breath out—the exasperated kind.

He stands up and leaves.

Fine. Whatever.

"Your mom's on her way, sweetie," Shelley says.

"*What?*" I sit up.

"I said your mom's on her way."

"Great," I mumble. Fabulous. Perfect. Mom will be here, giving me the angry-parent look. The one that makes me worry she'll keep me home because any day I might drop dead from diabetes.

Or worse. She'll cry.

"I swear, Kate. You're going to be grounded forever after this!" Jen crosses her legs on the floor. I'm still amazed Mom let her inside after the lecture I got in the car. Deena's staring at the TV, her eyes glazed over from being so sick.

"It's not my fault I'm diabetic."

"It *is* your fault that you're not keeping on top of it." She leans forward. "It's kind of a big deal."

"Thank you, *Mom*. I got the rant on the way home, okay?" I lean my back against the bottom of the couch. "I got the teeniest bit off, that's all. It's not my fault my stupid body wants to lie down every time I miscalculate or forget something."

"I'm sorry. And I know it's a big deal. But it's also not a big deal. I want you to be able to come out with us." Jen frowns.

"At least you're not heaving your guts out every few hours." Deena's eyes close again.

"At least your condition is temporary," I say. Maybe not the most sympathetic thing for me to bring up, but she knows it won't last forever.

"Yeah, well, Lane's not happy about the baby, okay? He said timing's off." The words come out in a mumble, and I'm almost not sure I heard her right.

Jen and I stare at each other, eyes wide.

"Sorry." Now I'm worried about why she's here, and how long she'll be staying if she and Lane aren't getting along. Which, yes, makes me a horrible sister.

12

AIDAN CONNELLY

I'm flipping dials in my new car while sitting in the driveway. Only took me three days to sell my Chevelle, and now I'm in a small two-door Volvo after driving a kickass car since I was sixteen. But the car's fast, and handles good.

The phone rings in my pocket, and I jerk it out to see a number I don't recognize. The letdown washes through me, and I'm in trouble because I wanted it to be Kate. She's a nice distraction. Okay, so I know it's more than that, but I'm trying to convince myself that's all there is.

The phone rings again. Instead of answering—I'm avoiding too many people—I wait for a new message.

Now it's safe to see who called.

"Hey…Connelly. It's Melinda…Pilot. I got your number from Roberts who called in the middle of the night the other night, but I was up. Again. Anyway, he said you're not too far from here, and I'd really like to see you. Please call…um, thanks…bye."

Her words crash into me. Push me under. Pull me down. I can't talk to her. I can't see her. Because it's not *just* her. It's the wife of the guy I watched die. The wife who cooked this monster barbecue for all of us and made us promise to bring her husband home safe. I don't know how to see her. How to face her.

I clutch my phone until my knuckles turn white, and nearly hurl it out the car window.

"How you liking the new wheels?" Foster leans into the car, and his face falls when we make eye contact. "What's up?"

I jump when I realize he's so close. "Melinda called."

"And?"

"I'm not that far down on my list yet." My body feels all numb and tingling.

"You need an outlet, Aidan."

"Wanna add something to my list? Because it's all feeling pretty fucked up right now." I toss the phone into the passenger's seat.

Foster pauses, probably ready to correct my language. "Nope. Just want to make sure you're okay, have somewhere for your energy to go."

"Okay. Thanks." Maybe I'll pick Kate up from school. That would be a nice place for my energy to go. And a hell of a lot easier than anything else I got going on.

The second Foster steps back I pull out of the driveway and head to Kate's school to wait for her day to finish.

Kate's whole face lights up, and it was worth it to come here for this. She's not even trying to hide how big her smile is, which just makes her even prettier.

"Hey."

This is exactly what I need right now. She's the perfect distraction. Perfect. Kate—the feel of her, the smell of her, it pretty much blocks out everything else.

"Hey." She walks toward me until she's about arm's length away.

Was our kiss a big deal? Should she be closer? Should I be doing something to get her closer?

"Are we okay?" she asks.

"Are we okay?" I'm confused.

Her cheeks flush. "I just wasn't sure, you know, how you felt about..."

"Kissing you?"

Her lips are pushing together, but not hard enough to keep in her happiness. I reach my hand out and take hers. She's pressed into me almost immediately, and I breathe her in.

"I like your new car." But her eyes aren't on the car—they're on me. And her stomach's against mine, and her breasts are pressing into me, and her hips are pressing into me.

"Really? 'Cause I think it's boring." And I can't believe I found words with how she feels next to me.

"It's an Edward Cullen car." I swear she's out of breath. Is it because of *me*?

"A what?"

"You know, *Twilight*. Edward Cullen. Sparkly vampire guy? Love interest in the Twilight movies? He drives this car exactly. At least in the first film."

"Oh. Great." I glance back, the guys are so going to give me crap over this—at least I didn't *know* and can give them crap over that. "Well it's fast, and most importantly, I can drive it."

"So, are you really giving me a ride home?"

"I might expect a small payment, you know, maybe..."

But her lips are on mine before I can finish. This girl makes me crazy. She's pressing our bodies even more tightly together as I lean on my car.

"Wanna show me the inside?" She's out of breath, and her cheek is on mine until her lips hit my neck.

"Definitely."

It's a bit tricky maneuvering into the backseat with only one arm. I keep reaching out to support myself or to touch her, and nothing's there. This is going to be frustrating, but Kate doesn't seem to notice. She's pulling me to her so hard that there really isn't time for me to notice what I can and can't do. I half fall on her and she laughs, leans forward, and bites my lower lip.

I'm not sure how much time we spend kissing in my car, but it's like I can't stop. Can't take my mouth off of hers as long as she wants to move with me. My one arm is wrapped around her, holding her to me, and it's okay. Not ideal because I want to touch her arm, stroke her hair and still keep a hand on her smooth back, but it's still good.

"Wow." She leans the tiniest bit away from me. "There's more room in the backseat than I would have guessed."

My face pulls into a smile, nothing but me and Kate, and I don't have to care or worry about anything else right now. I push her hair off her face. "You're pretty."

Her cheeks are immediately pink. I love embarrassing her.

"And you make me really like white t–shirts."

"What?" I glance down. "Is that totally boring?"

Her eyes aren't on my face anymore. Her fingers trace patterns on my chest, and down my stomach. These light little touches push waves through me. Waves of feeling Kate. Waves of distraction.

"Careful." I'm trying to tease, but my voice isn't working right because I want her. Really want her. And this is not the place or the time or the way we should be doing anything more than what we're doing. "You have me really turned on."

"Sorry." She jerks her hand away.

I grab her hand, and slide our fingers together. Something about how small her hands are makes me feel stronger, tougher, good. "Don't be."

Our eyes meet again. Our lips meet again for not nearly long enough. "If I'm not home soon, Mom's going to flip."

"Okay." But part of me doesn't want to move. I want to hang with her in the backseat of my car. We could talk. We could kiss. Maybe I could show her how turned on I get around her.

Her hands go up the back of my shirt, and the heat of her about makes me insane with how I want her. I slide my hand under her shirt, and up her smooth side. She gasps and pulls me closer. Kisses me harder. We're both totally out of breath when she sits back.

"Maybe you could pick me up again sometime?" She's not looking at me, but at my lips.

Pick her up again? Like a routine? That thought sends a prick into me. I'm not sure what it is, but this is the whole attached, boyfriend thing I'm not sure I can do. I don't know *how* to do. But I look over her sweet face, and remember her hands on me, and know I'll happily come back for more.

"I'm sure I'll end up back here sometime."

Her face falls, just slightly before she kisses me again and crawls out of the back.

Guess I'm going to have to be a little more careful about what I say to her.

※

Okay. I've got the packet from the community college spread out around me on the counter, and the History Channel's playing my favorite show—*Mail Call*. I'm trying to get excited about something, but it's not happening. I'm supposed to see the counselor tomorrow, and I have no idea what we're going to accomplish if I walk in with a blank head. There was a brief time I thought about teaching, but school wasn't easy for me, so it's probably not the best option. My career was taken from me, and it's a hard thing to get over.

I turn off the TV, and shift my weight on the stool, hoping that it'll help me focus.

A knock at my door rescues me from my thoughts.

"Come in!"

Jen steps in. I'm pretty sure this is a first.

"What's up?" I ask as I drop my pen. It still feels weird to hold the thing with my left hand. My handwriting is like a second grader's scrawl—another thing that goes on the list of things I can't do anymore.

She closes the door but doesn't really move into the room. I'm on a barstool in the tiny kitchen waiting for her to say something.

"About Kate." She sighs and folds her arms, so I know it's probably going to be something I don't want to hear.

My nerves settle in. "Yeah?"

"She..." But now her brows are all pulled down, and I don't think I've ever seen Jen look anything but put together.

I sit and let her be nervous.

"Look, she's my best friend, and..." She pauses for so long I start to get frustrated.

"*And?*" I don't want to have this conversation. I have no idea how to be a good boyfriend to anyone, especially right now, but I don't want to let her go. Maybe I'm hopelessly selfish for wanting to be around her, or maybe we both need distraction. I don't know, but I do know I don't want to talk about it. I don't really want anything to taint how good she feels against me.

"She has a lot going on right now."

"Don't we all." It takes conscious effort for me to not throw the pen into a window or against the wall.

"Right. I..." She pushes out air. "I'm sorry. I know you're family, but I barely know you and I'm—"

"Looking out for your friend." I'm trying to keep out what I'd like to tell her, and I'd kind of like to tell her to butt out. She's the one who set us up in the beginning.

"Yeah, um, thanks." She starts to turn, but stops.

"Something else?" I start to fold my arms, but again, one fucking arm doesn't cross well. And I have no idea what exactly Jen wants from me.

"We used to use this place once in a while for movies and stuff, and since you like her, I thought maybe we could do a movie night here or something?"

"Is this 'cause you want to spy on me with your friend or because you're trying to tell me it's okay that I like her?" Mostly I'm confused as hell.

"Umm...both?"

I chuckle, and her whole body relaxes.

"Thanks for being honest," I say.

"Yeah. I guess let me know when's good for you."

"Friday?" Do I sound too anxious? I'm not sure.

"Probably Friday, yeah. Thanks." She gives me a brief wave before walking out the door.

Kate has a lot going on? What can possibly be going on? Also, she didn't seem very hesitant in the back of my car. I mean, I thought a kiss would be nice, but that was...well, it was enough to push down some of the walls I've kept up between us, that's for sure. At least I have Friday night to look forward to.

13

Kate Walker

Deena and I sit comatose in front of the TV. I'm still in shock over how Aidan made me feel in the back of his car. I've never been that way with a guy. I've never felt like that, like I wanted him to go further, and it's crazy because I barely know him. And now I have this nervous anticipation over Friday and watching a movie at what's sort of his house.

In Jen's (now Aidan's) small garage apartment was the furthest Shelton and I ever got—on a *movie night*. And that wasn't all that far. Probably about on par with the backseat of Aidan's new car. What's with me?

"I'm so nervous." Deena turns toward me, looking a little less pale than normal. I don't think she's been throwing up as much, but I've been pre-occupied.

"What's up?" Do I want to know?

"Lane's coming in this weekend." She starts chomping on a fingernail—something I haven't seen her do since she was in high school.

"And that's good, right?" How long has she been here and not seen him?

"I hope so."

"Well, I'm crashing at Jen's on Friday. Movie night."

Deena's eyes are hard on me. "Aidan?"

I try so hard not to react, breathing slowly, and anything I can think of, but my stupid grin spreads anyway.

"Be careful with that boy." She raises a brow.

"What boy?" Mom sets down two laundry baskets, and I can tell by the look on her face that not only is she about to butt in on our conversation, but she'll want me to fold laundry as well.

"Aidan." Deena grins poking me in the side.

This is kind of a dead giveaway that Deena and I may have talked about him once or twice, which is going to make it really difficult for me to convince Mom that he and I are no big deal— even though I don't know what he and I are.

"He's two years older than you." Mom rubs her temple like she always does when stressed.

I push out a laugh. "Mom we've only..." Only what? Groped each other in the back of his car? Twice? Had a few sort of amazing moments while babysitting? Had a great day of driving around in silence while I skipped school? Can't really talk to Mom about that.

"Only?" Mom prompts.

"Seen each other a couple of times. It's not a big deal." But as the words come out, I kind of think it is a big deal. At least it feels like a big deal.

"You split with Shelton not long ago and you two were together for quite a while." Mom's doing her eyebrow raised thingy that says—we both know this might not be the best idea.

I nod. "Yeah, but we were headed to different colleges anyway." Because I'm getting out of here to join Jen at USC.

"And what are Aidan's plans?"

"Mom! Seriously? I'm not marrying the guy! I've met up with him a couple of times and both were with groups of people!" No one else knows about the pick-up from school or the fabulous kissing in the back of his car. Just us. Us. Him and me. Me and him. His lips. My lips. His hand. My hands. And then I let out a giggle— not what I should be doing to convince Mom to let me spend time with him.

"Okay. Just remember that he's dealing with a lot." She frowns.

I pull in a breath and try on my best serious face. "Yeah. He lost his arm and a good friend. I get it."

"You get it?" Her brows rise in disbelief.

No one could really understand what he's been through, but he seems to be doing fine.

"Mom!" I'm completely exasperated. "When have you ever asked me so much about someone I may or may not even like?"

Mom shifts her weight to one leg. "Be careful. The age difference worries me, and so does his situation. I want you to know where I stand before you get involved."

"Okay." I fold my arms, and want to tell her that I think we're done, but it probably wouldn't be the smartest move.

"Mom?" Deena turns toward her. "Kate's going to be in college next year. Two years is nothing."

Wait. What? My sister who was worried a minute ago, is now okay with this?

Mom sighs and her eyes are on me. "We trust you, Kate."

I can't believe she's pulling that card. *"Mom."*

"Don't forget to check your blood-sugar while you're out with friends. You tend to forget." She does this weird almost moving thing, but pausing long enough to maybe show me that I'm lucky for getting off so easy because she has more to say. I'm not sure that I got off easy at all.

Since I'm still practically on house arrest after my doctor's appointment, and then my high blood sugar read at school, Jen's very nicely visiting me between all her student government/over-achiever activities and make-out sessions with her boyfriend.

Our legs stretch out in front of us as we sit in front of my bed. I'm not sure why, but it always feels easier to talk when we're on the floor.

"Have you and Toby had sex?" I whisper. "You two have been... together a lot lately." I'm assuming she would have told me, but we haven't seen each other much the past few days.

"Not yet." She bites her lower lip as she holds in her smile.

"But you're thinking about it," I urge.

She nods. "It's like I'm scared, but it's Toby, so I'm not scared, you know? I mean, I know he's going away to school, and the thought of us not staying together sucks, but we're both smart enough to know it could go either way. I'm at the point where I know I love him, and I know he's always going to be the guy I loved in high school no matter what happens over the next four years in college, and…"

"And you trust him and want him to be your first," I finish.

"Yeah. Pretty much."

"You guys still have all summer." Only I'm pretty sure he's staying in Oregon for college, and Jen and I are leaving.

"I know." She smiles. "I know there's a chance we could make it, but I realized it doesn't matter either way because I love him right now."

"Wow." I lean my head on her shoulder. "He's pretty awesome."

"And you seem recovered."

"From what?" I sit up.

She laughs. "Shelton."

"Oh. Right." I let out a breath. "It still sucks, but mostly because I wish he would have been honest with me, you know?"

"Because honesty is a big deal." There's this authority/mother tone in her voice that I'm not liking.

I lean away. "What?"

"Aidan really needs to know you're diabetic if you guys are going to keep hanging out." She purses her lips. "If you get all wonky it would be nice for him to know how to help."

My jaw flexes in frustration. "I know. It's just. It's so nice to be around someone who isn't always watching me for some sign of weakness. Does that make sense? I mean, especially right now with this whole text every blood sugar read to Mom and Dad. I'm tired of it all."

Jen puts her arm around my shoulder. "It makes perfect sense, but the longer you wait, the more awkward it's going to be."

I nod. "Yeah. Okay. I'll find a good time."

Jen shakes her head. "You're turning it into a big deal, Kate. Just tell him you carry a monster purse so you can check your blood sugar. No biggie."

No biggie. Right. Because it's not her that's carrying half a pharmacy everywhere she goes.

14

AIDAN CONNELLY

Even though I'm thinking about Kate a lot, I'm also trying not to set up some ridiculous thing where I'm picking her up every day. I almost text her four times to say I'll get her, which I can't make a habit of, so I jump in my car and head to Mom's house to prevent starting that whole high school smothering thing.

I pick up McDonald's for the twins on my way, figuring that should buy us at least a few minutes of talk time, and maybe buy my mom a sanity moment.

Mom opens the door immediately after I pull up and gives me grateful smile as she takes the two Happy Meal boxes from my hands.

In about two minutes Mom and I are on the couch together, while the twins stuff themselves with McDonald's.

"How's Kate?" She jumps right in, which I guess is good since we're always short on time.

I suck in a breath. "She's…" And now I'm smiling. "I like her, but don't know how—" *To be a boyfriend.* Or if I can be right now.

"How what?"

"I don't know what she wants or how to give it to her, or if I should, or if I should be leaving her alone." It's all sort of a mess, and I probably shouldn't be thinking about it so much. I have a lot of other stuff that really needs to be sorted out.

"You really, really like her." Mom sits sideways on her couch, resting an elbow on the back.

"Why do you say that?" I slouch lower so I look more relaxed than I feel, but there's probably no point in doing that in front of Mom. She always sees through me.

"Because you're putting her first. Not you. If you didn't like her as much, you'd just be enjoying yourself and taking what she can give." Mom's lips are pressed together, making her look even happier because she's trying not to.

"Maybe. I feel like I'm still getting to know her, even though she just says the most random things. Like I get the surface her, and not the real her." It's something I don't know if I fully noticed until I say it out loud. The cool thing is that I want to know her better, and she doesn't make me too nervous like some of the girls I've been around. Maybe this is a place where our age difference will help me.

"Do you want the real her?" Mom asks.

"Yes and no." It's scary. And it shouldn't be because she's just a girl.

"Then you're being as careful as you need to be." Mom rubs the back of her finger up my cheek. She's done this since I started shaving. It's her way of doing something over the top *Mom* while still showing she knows how grown up I am.

"She's so much younger, you know?"

"I'm close with my sister and I've spent a bit of time around Kate. I think she's lived a lot more life than she's letting on." And something passes behind my mom's eyes that makes me wonder if she knows something I don't.

"Maybe. And now I feel like a total girl for over-thinking the whole thing."

"I'm glad you are. The only thing that I'm going to warn you about with her age is to let her decide how fast you two move, okay? No pressuring the girl, or going too far too fast." And this is the warning look. The one that says I might be in deep shit if I screw up.

I can feel a smile spread as I think about her hands under my shirt in the back of my car.

The back of Mom's hand slaps my chest as she smiles.

"What was *that* for?" I laugh and hold my arm between us.

"It's all over your face. Time to realize you like her a lot, and be careful, okay?"

"Yeah." I nod as it all sinks in. "Okay."

I step into the guidance counselor's office at the community college, having no idea how Mr. Burn might be able to help me.

The guy behind the desk is as buried underneath glasses, beard, and button-up shirt as his desk is in papers.

This was supposed to be my first thing, but I don't even know where I am on the list anymore, only that Kate's now definitely on it—in as many places as I can fit her without jumping into a relationship too fast. Though, it might be too late for that.

"What can I do for you, Specialist Connelly?" He smiles, using my rank.

"Not specialist anymore, Mr. Burn." I shake my head a bit surprised.

"I won't agree to that." He chuckles. "Sergeant Burn, 756th Infantry."

And I relax. This guy will actually sort of "get" some part of me, even if he looks like a disaster.

"Nasty scrape you got there." He gestures to my arm.

I grin. "Yeah. Scrape."

"What can I do for ya?" He leans forward resting his elbows on stacks of papers.

"Tell me what I should do with my life?" I chuckle. Only laughing is about the last thing I feel like doing.

"What were you thinking of doing after the Army?" He gestures to a seat, and I take it.

"The Army."

"Well, shit. Sorry soldier." He flips a pen over in his hand a few times.

The guy's cussing. Understanding. Not looking defeated by me being completely clueless.

"If that's the case then my guess is that you want some sort of end goal, something to make all this school crap worthwhile." He spins to his computer and starts hitting keys.

"Yes, sir."

"I can put you through some aptitude tests, and tell you where your talents lie, but I'm not sure that'll help you, Connelly." He spins back to me.

"So…"

"I want you to not think about school and classes and all that. I want you to think about something that'll really make you feel good. Here." He pats his chest. "Or pick something that'll make you a boatload of money." He chuckles at his own joke.

"You don't blow smoke." He's definitely more straightforward than I expected.

"Doesn't really do either of us any favors, does it?" he asks.

"No, sir."

"Here's what we'll do for now. I'm going to hand pick some really great teachers, put you in classes that I think are a little more interesting than average, and maybe you'll have an epiphany sometime during your first semester."

It sounds great, but…"What if I don't?" I ask.

He chuckles. "Then we'll hope for it the next semester, or the next, or at least soon enough that you can graduate in four-ish years with a degree in *something*."

This is not what I want to hear, and I feel more defeated than when I stepped in.

"Aidan?"

"Yeah?"

"Sometimes trying to focus and think on something makes it even more elusive. Think on it, but don't hurt your brain on it, and I bet it'll come to you." He leans back and rests an ankle on his knee. At least he knows how to cross his legs like a man.

"I'll add it to the list."

He cocks a brow.

"Long story." I sigh.

Mr. Burn frowns. "I feel like I haven't helped you, and I really hate that."

"Nah. You've given me someone to talk to, Sergeant." I stand up.

"Okay. Come back in if you think I can help with something else." He jumps to his feet and we shake over his disaster of a desk.

"I'll be back. You're still on my list." And now I gotta figure out what's coming up next. I'm pretty sure the guys are coming home, and I really should be more excited to see them all again. But tomorrow night is my next date with Kate, so I'm pretty sure I'm going to slide her into the next slot on my list.

15

Kate Walker

As I step up to Jen's house, Shelton's car is here. Toby's car is here and two others. What's going on? I'm not into a big group for movie night, especially since I'm sleeping over so I can't just leave if it gets weird. I also really don't want to sit in the same room with both Aidan and Shelton. It's way too soon to be anything but awkward. And how could I snuggle against Aidan the way I want with Shelton there? He might not have any issue parading Tamara around, but I couldn't do it.

"Hey, Kate." Aidan steps out of his apartment and lightly jogs down the stairs. Red T-shirt today, making his hair look even blonder. The red also sets off his tanned skin and blue eyes and my heart leaps a few times.

Aidan looks like I want him to. Easy. Comfortable.

Aidan walks like Aidan wants to walk. Like Aidan wants to dress. No pretension. No nothing but Aidan. His emotions on his face, the straight-backed, forward movement that stuck with him from the military.

"Are you here? Do you need me today? Or should I leave you with your thoughts?" Aidan teases as he moves in close.

"I'm good. You?" I take a step so we're touching—chest, hips, a small part of my thighs.

"Yeah." His fingers slide along my hand.

I immediately slide my hand through his and my body and mostly my lips hope for…but I don't get to finish the thought before his lips touch mine again. The way I feel next to him scares me. Like I'm too comfortable, want more of him. Well any girl would want more than that little soft kiss.

And my needles don't matter, and my overly strict parents don't matter, and Shelton doesn't matter. Just Aidan. Okay. And his lips.

"You're stubbly." I pull away and rub my finger across his chin.

"Sorry, I got busy today and didn't shave."

I kiss his chin, just to feel the prickly hairs on my lips again, and smile.

"We ordered pizza," he says. "Jen insisted on ordering a salad with it—"

"Oh, good." Pizza is a pain to count carbs for.

He rolls his eyes. "Not you too."

"Kate!"

I spin around just in time to see Shelton give me his perfectly placed, white-toothed smile.

My heart drops. Oh. This is nice. I'm standing between them.

"You look like you're feeling better today." He jogs down the steps from Jen's front door, and once again the difference between the two guys is a bit staggering. Perfectly pressed and poised Shelton versus relaxed and comfortable Aidan. Why was I so broken up over Shelton?

"Oh, right. Yeah. I'm fine," I spit out, realizing that he's referring to the stupid shot he had to give me. The one I'd rather Aidan not know about. Not yet.

Aidan's eyes are on me, and I hope the conversation keeps rolling so nothing needs to be discussed.

"What are you guys up to tonight?" Shelton asks. His gaze glances down to my hand laced with Aidan's.

Toby, Jen, and the rest of student government come out of her house, and slowly wander down from the porch.

"Movie night," Aidan says.

Shelton freezes. He and I both know what happens on movie night. We pick out one movie we all want to watch, and another that no one wants to watch so we can make out. Shelton's eyes snap back and forth between Aidan and me a few more times.

"I'm going to go check on pizza." I smile back at Aidan, touching his stomach briefly, because my fingers apparently have a mind of their own, and I really need to avoid looking at Shelton and jog up the steps before anyone asks me anything else about school and shots.

"Hey, Kate!" Jen's mom smiles from across the vast entry. "The pizza should be here any minute."

"Oh. Thanks." That was way too fast. And easy. Now I'll have to go back outside and try to make nice. Maybe Shelton's gone.

"Hey, Kate?" Shelton's voice.

Okay. Maybe not. I turn slowly. "What's up?" I can sound casual. No big deal.

"Are you um...?"

I'm desperately trying to hold in my smile, because of course Shelton would want to know about Aidan. He's always liked being in on the details of people.

"Dating that guy?"

Jen's mom glances at me and then walks from the room. She's always been really awesome at giving us our privacy. My parents could totally learn a lesson or two from them.

"*That guy* is Aidan. He's Jen's cousin, and—"

"I know who he is." Shelton shakes his head in impatience.

Right. I'm already annoyed. "Oh. Sorry. So you called him *that guy* for a reason?"

Shelton rolls his eyes like a parent. Like we both know what he's talking about and I'm being juvenile.

"We've gone out a few times." I nod.

"He's not. I mean, he's not the kind of guy I figured you'd go for."

I laugh. I mean, what else am I supposed to do?

"Kate? Pizza's here!" Aidan steps in the front door and almost runs into Shelton. His eyes go from me to Shelton and back to me a few times.

This is all about as perfectly awkward as anyone would imagine, and I'm ready for it to be over.

"Thanks." I step around Shelton while trying on my best sympathetic smile—the one he's been giving me since Tamara. "We'll see you later."

The door closes behind us.

"You okay in there?" Aidan whispers.

"Totally fine, but I'm glad you stepped in anyway." I wrap my arm around his waist and lean in and the beginnings of nervous anticipation about our night slide in.

Aidan kisses the side of my head, pulling me toward him. Okay. Aidan. I can do this. Whatever *this* is. Better. Much, much, better.

Toby and Jen forgot that we usually actually watch the first movie, and they're all over each other on the other side of the enormous sectional. She wasn't kidding when she said something about them being close to going all the way. Okay. So they are sort of watching the movie. But then he'll kiss her or she'll kiss him, and I'm trying not to look, but come *on*.

I'm not sure what to do. I mean, kissing Aidan is awesome, but I'm lying in the crook of his arm and that's awesome too. Also, it suddenly feels too personal to kiss him like that in front of them. And it's not that I never kissed Shelton in front of Toby and Jen, it's that I never lost control while kissing Shelton, and I'm not certain I could kiss Aidan without losing control.

I have no idea what the movie's about because I can't pay attention with Jen and Toby making out on the end of the couch.

I'm leaning against Aidan, whose warmth is pushing into me and spinning my brain into a place I don't remember it being before. One that makes me feel a bit like a guy because I'm thinking about him the way I think most guys think about girls. *What can I touch? How do we start? When can we kiss without it being forced or weird?*

"You wanna go for a walk?" I whisper.

"Yes." He breathes out this huge sigh of relief and immediately stands.

Jen starts and half jumps away from Toby, wiping her mouth. Hysterical.

"We're going for a walk. You two have an hour. We'll knock before we come in." Aidan smirks as he holds the door open for me.

He takes my hand as we hit the bottom of the stairs.

"Hi." I squeeze his hand in mine.

"Hi." His smile is warm and complete.

"It's just been…"

"Awkward?" he suggests.

"Yes. With Shelton asking about you, and Jen and Toby…"

"Good thing she's not my sister or I'd have to kick his ass." Aidan chuckles.

I look up at his straight jaw line and blue eyes, wanting to kiss him like I did when he held me at the parking lot of my school.

He glances over his shoulder. "I think we're out of sight of the house, now."

"Wha—"

But I don't get to finish before his lips are on mine. Soft enough to turn me to mush and then hard enough to tighten my whole body in response.

His hand rests firmly on my lower back, holding us together. There's a tingle of desperation in his kiss that makes my arms pull on him harder.

"Wow." I breathe out as his lips leave mine.

"Yeah, wow." He rests his arm over my shoulder, and I lean into him as we start walking again.

"Thanks for getting out of there." It feels good to be alone with him.

"It's hard. Only having one hand. Like I kiss you and I want to hold you and touch you, and I can't. Like I can only touch you in one place at a time."

"No." I shake my head and stop. Aidan stops with me.

His arm slides down and I take his hand.

"I'm in AP Biology. Just by holding hands we're touching in millions or trillions of tiny little places." I step closer. Maybe that thought should creep me out, but it doesn't—not when thinking about Aidan. Though, he might think I'm a total weirdo for bringing this up.

"And how about now?" He steps in until our stomach, chest, and legs all touch.

"Even more places." But I'm breathless again, and his lips are soft, and then he chuckles.

"You. Kate. Are very distracting."

And he is too. In such a good way. "You make this easy," I say as we start to walk again.

"What?"

"Being with you is easy." Which is exactly opposite of everything else I'm dealing with.

"Good. I mean, it is for me too, and I have a lot going on right now."

"You must." I really want to know more about him. I want to know about the way he grew up and why he joined the military and what he wants to do with his life.

Our eyes catch, and I know he knows I'm asking him without asking.

"Starting college, not having any idea what I want to do. My unit comes home from Afghanistan any day now, and I haven't checked my email because I don't want to know when they come home because I'm not sure I want to see them."

"Why not?"

"Because they get to keep doing it." His jaw flexes, highlighting everything I find sexy about his face, but it also sends a pang of sadness through me to see the frustration.

"You really wanted to be a soldier." Everyone I know that signed up did it for the medical (pregnant girlfriend/wife) or for school, or because they had nothing else going for them. But Aidan really wanted it. It's crushing really. Not only did he lose his arm but also his job.

He nods. Then he tells me about his dad dying so young, and about joining the military not long after his mom got married again. He talks about how crazy her life is with the kids and how lost he sometimes feels.

All of the surface stuff I've been feeling for him digs deeper, and this isn't just flirtation and wanting to touch more of him. This is real. I open my mouth to say something about my diabetes, but I'm not ready to lose him as someone who doesn't know.

"Sorry, I guess I dumped a lot on you." A corner of his mouth pulls up, and I notice that as his hair's gotten slightly longer, there's also a small amount of curl in there. It's more noticeable just above his ears. "I totally didn't mean to."

"No, it's okay. Totally okay." We stop in the street. "I like knowing you better."

"And what about Kate?" He kisses my forehead.

"I..." And I almost do it. I almost talk to him about lying in the hospital after passing out in school not having any idea why I'd been so exhausted. How out of control of my life I feel, but how I can't take control of it. But just because I loved hearing about him, doesn't mean that he'd love hearing about me.

"Normal boring teenage stuff." I shrug. "My sister is having a hard time with her pregnancy and my parents are over-protective, and I have no idea what I want to do in college." *And I'm totally falling for you.*

"Well, that makes two of us." He smiles again and kisses me, and as his lips touch mine, I realize that one of the reasons it's less scary to be close to him is that he's done all of this before. He may fumble a bit because he's not used to having one arm, but he's been with girls before. Has to have. And he kisses and holds me with more confidence and wanting than anyone's ever kissed me before.

His arm wraps around me tighter, and our kiss deepens making me push my body harder against him.

We could. I could. He wouldn't even have to know it was my first time, and it wouldn't be some huge deal, it would be him and me, and *wow*. I could actually do it. It's a little scary, but doable. Going all the way didn't feel like it was even in the realm of near future for me until now.

"I think their time's up," he whispers.

"Agreed."

We don't talk much on the way back. I lean into the warmth of him and we stop to kiss once in a while, but every time we do both of us get so caught up in each other that we're out of breath by the time we get moving again.

We open the door to see Toby and Jen standing on the other side.

"I'm going to walk Toby home," Jen says as she gives her shirt a tug.

"I'll see you in the morning." I let my eyes meet hers so she'll maybe catch on that I'd rather not be disturbed, even though the thought of it sends these nervous flutters through me.

Her brows go up a bit. "See you in the morning."

And then they leave. Us. Alone.

I don't even wait for an awkward pause. I turn from the door and kiss Aidan with everything I have. He answers back, nearly picking me up off the ground as his arm wraps tightly around my lower back.

"Can we go to your room?" I can't believe I said that.

He laughs. "Let me try something."

Before I can react I'm over his shoulder, his arm holding me firmly in place.

"Aidan!" I laugh and hit his back.

"Your idea, Kate."

He's still grinning when he sets me down, but now we're in *his* *room*. The only light filters through the white blinds.

I suck in a breath because everything's different but the same because it's still him and it's still me. Whatever movie's playing filters in, but I can't make out words. Its just noise that doesn't matter.

"You're amazing. You feel amazing." He leans in slowly, and kisses my cheek.

I'm holding my breath. "I'm totally average. I'm always just trying to keep up or catch up or something."

"Kate." His lips nearly touch mine as he talks. "There is nothing, *nothing* average about you."

It's simple, but probably one of the best compliments I've

gotten in my life. I move my hands up his chest and around his neck, but then I slide them down, unsure if I should run my hand over where his arm used to be. Is that okay? Would it make him uncomfortable? Would it hurt?

"Can I see your arm?" I ask.

Instead of answering, he pulls his T-shirt over his head and drops it to the floor, and I forget to look at where his arm used to be. I'm looking at his chest, his tight abs, his back, and whoa, wow. Shelton's toned, sort of. He's thin, but Aidan's built like...I guess he's built like a man. Different. Nervous tingles hit me in the pit of my stomach. A man. Older, more experience in life, I'm sure in love, in everything.

"That bad?" he asks.

"I wasn't looking at your arm." Stupid, *stupid* lack of filter!

"Are you checking me out, Kate?" he teases.

But I don't have it in me to tease. Not right now. I run my hand over his chest, down his stomach and even have the guts to slide my fingertips into the front of his jeans.

"Hmm." The deepness of his voice vibrates through me.

I tug on his waistband as I back up. When I sit on his bed, he sits next to me. Close enough that the warmth of his body hits me in millions and billions of little places.

His shoulder is covered in welted red scars, but doesn't look as strange as I thought it would. There are tiny marks down his side to the top of his jeans, and also up his neck and under his ear.

I can feel his pulse quicken, and his eyes are almost wary as he watches me. Maybe he's worried about what I'll think. What I see.

"Is it...?" He shakes his head once, and I'm realizing that Aidan does head-shakes like my dad does breathe-outs. This one makes him seem uncertain. "Is my arm weird? I mean. Is it—?"

"It's fine. Good." I'm not making sense, and I don't mean to, but my fingers are on him, tracing the scarring, wondering what it would be like to be part of something so insane. So real.

"How did it happen?" The words just come out.

"Walking on perimeter patrol. Doing nothing. They hid it well. Pilot took the worst of it." His voice is quieter than a whisper.

"What happened to him?" And again, once the words are out I realize how stupid I am for asking him.

"Torn apart. They couldn't put him back together. He was my sergeant."

I don't know what it means for Pilot to be his sergeant, but it doesn't really matter. What matters is that he was next to someone who died. I rest my two hands on his bare shoulder and see the sadness—though that word doesn't begin to describe what's on his face. "I'm sorry."

"Me too." His fingers start to trace around on my shoulder and arm, sending shivers through me.

I lean forward and kiss his shoulder, as close to the scarring as I dare because I'm part uncomfortable, and I think he is too. My lips touch the red marks on his collarbone, and then his neck, and then without thinking I pull my shirt over my head and drop it to the floor. It should be dark enough to hide any tiny bits of bruising from my shots.

Now I'm sitting here. Bra. No shirt. In front of Aidan, and I'm not nervous at all. Okay. I'm terrified, but I want it way more than I'm scared. He seems a lot more exposed than I feel—the stump of his arm so visible. His experiences hanging between us.

His eyes are on mine. "Are you sure you—?"

"I felt overdressed." I try to make my voice teasing, but this is all too close for that, and I'm sure made me sound weird.

"Maybe I'll drop my pants next." His voice is uncertain, but there's a hint of question.

"Maybe I'll drop mine," I say completely breathless. Okay, so there are definitely nerves, but I trust him. I think about what he shared with me on our walk, and how I feel when we touch. Now I'm thinking how much better this is because we didn't plan it or anything. We're here, and I'm pretty sure it's going to happen.

His hand cups my face and he gently brings our foreheads together. "The second you say pause, we pause or we stop."

No, no. This isn't right. I want him to treat me like anyone. "Why are you being so careful with me?"

"Because I like you. A lot. And because both my mom and Foster really like you and gave me a lecture on being nice, and—"

I cut him off with my lips and pull him on top of me. No one else needs to be in this room but us. Fire races through me as our skin connects. I can stop this, at any point I can stop this, but as we continue to kiss, and my body continues to crave more of him, I wonder why on earth I'd want to stop anything.

"I've never done this with one arm. I mean, I might need some help," he whispers between kisses.

I help him with his pants and he chuckles this nervous little chuckle because he can obviously dress himself, and I let out a nervous laugh because I've never let someone see me naked before. Not even in the dark. And definitely not for something like this.

And we're both frantic, but absorbing every moment all at the same time. His fingers trace every curve, every part of me. He touches me until my body half explodes and I feel flattened and high in something incredible I didn't used to understand.

As I lie next to him still gasping for air, he fumbles with a condom until I find the guts to reach out and help, and *touch him* and we're actually going to do this, and I still want it and his weight's on me again, and there's pressure, but he's slow, and I still don't want to pause and then his hips are rocking against mine and I never, ever, ever want our night to stop ever.

In what could be hours or minutes or days I'm resting in the crook of his arm, exhausted, sweaty, and a bit in disbelief. My toes touch the top of his feet, and our knees are close, but not exact. Our legs tangle together, and the hair on his legs touches mine, but it feels good, manly, and his abs and chest. I love his abs and chest, and I can't stop my fingers from tracing the contours over and over.

"Join me in the shower?" he asks as his fingertips slide up my spine spreading goose bumps over my skin.

I feel the blush creeping in and can't look at him.

"You're seriously blushing about rinsing off after that?" he chuckles as he runs his hand through my hair.

"I'll wait here." I need to do a quick blood sugar check anyway.

He kisses me again, rolls over, and walks to his bathroom without a stitch of clothing on. And yes. I stare. Wow. I just had sex with Aidan Connelly. Talk about best distraction ever.

16

AIDAN CONNELLY

The hot shower pelts my body. I can't believe I just had sex with Kate. How does this fit in with Foster and my mother's warning? And Jen's? Well. And my *own*.

It was her idea, though. Not mine. I didn't take pants off. And it was easily the best ever for me—though doing it on a cot or in a bathroom while rushing isn't exactly recommended. The lack of room...of time...I dry off and can't wrap my towel around my waist with only one arm. The right side falls down before I can tuck. Hell.

My hips swing around trying to get both sides of the towel in one hand, and even though I'm alone, I'm starting to feel a bit ridiculous. Nope. It was one thing to walk away from her naked, but it feels different to walk back into the room while flopping around. I lean against the sink to hold one side of the towel, while I tuck the other side back in the front. I slowly lean away and the towel...*stays*. Victory.

When I open the door, Kate's lying on her stomach in one of my white T-shirts and her panties making my heart race again because she's here. She's so beautiful. Slim, long legs, sweet smile, and she still looks almost embarrassed, but she's also staring at me in the way I love.

Instead of heading to my dresser for pajamas or at least boxers, I kneel down next to my bed, putting our faces close together.

"Thank you. I mean, that seems like a really weird thing to say, but I feel amazing."

Her eyes glance down. "Me too."

I touch her chin until she meets my eyes again with pink cheeks, and then I kiss her. This is real. This is all so real, but it's really, really good. She is definitely more than a distraction. Or starting to be. Or since we had sex, maybe we're way past distraction. I'm not sure how this works. "I'm glad you don't have to leave."

"Me too."

I slide on a pair of pajama pants, glad I have practice with one hand, and see her watching me again out of the corner of my eye. It's good to have a pretty girl watching me like this. I climb back in with her, use my arm to bring us together, and fall asleep harder and faster than I have in a long time.

Kate stirs next to me at sometime around seven in the morning. I grab her waist and pull her closer. "Where do you think you're going?" I whisper.

"Trust me. Foster always does an early morning check."

"Oh." I pull my arm back. "Do you wanna stay in here, and I'll go…" I feel a bit like a jerk if I make her sleep on the couch.

"Definitely not. Jen's crashed out there, so I'm going to join her. I think that's what he's sort of expecting."

I rest my hand on her neck, lean in, and kiss her cheek. She pushes on my chest, keeping me in bed as she stands. She grins as she picks up her monster bag, and steps out of the room. I crash again.

I stumble into the house around eleven. Kate was gone when I woke up, but my pillow smelled like her, which made me remember our night, her lean body underneath me, and that was a nice way to wake up.

"Where's Kate?" I ask Jen as I step inside.

"Her sister's husband came back into town today. She had to run home." There's a tinge of annoyance to her voice that I'm trying to ignore.

"Oh." I rub my hand up and down my face a few times to wipe away some of the sleep when my cell phone rings. I answer without thinking.

"Hello?"

"Where the fuck are you, Connelly?"

"Rob?"

"Who the hell else would it be?"

"I…" Confused doesn't even begin to describe.

"You sound like you partied harder than we did last night!"

"You're home?" Which is a stupid question seeing as he's calling me during the day and said something about partying.

"Got in yesterday morning. Looked for you *everywhere*. I can't figure out how the hell you didn't make it."

"Shit. Sorry. I'm behind on email." My body still feels all relaxed after my night last night.

"Come up, Con." And I know by his voice that he'd never admit it but it was an asshole thing of me to not show. He's been my friend for too long for me to not be there.

"Yeah. I will. For sure."

Jen's scowling at me, her arms crossed in front of her. Maybe I should take care of this.

"I'll call you later."

"Later like next month later? Or later as in today?" He's teasing, but there's irritation in there too. I can't really blame him. I've never brushed him off before. Not like I have been.

"You sound like a woman. Later today."

I hang up, my eyes still on Jen's.

"What's up?" I ask only I probably don't want to know.

"You guys had scx last night?" Jen raises a brow. Her jaw is clenched and her arms are crossed. A sure sign that I've messed up.

"Uh…" I look around. This is not something I want her parents in on.

"They're gone," she snaps.

"Yeah, what…" I'm lost here.

"You need to do something for her. I can't believe you *slept* this morning! You should have been like, making breakfast or something! Snuggling with her on the couch! I don't know."

I have no idea what to do with this attack. I don't know Jen well enough to yell back, but I'm starting to wish I did. This is none of her damn business. None.

Her brows are practically touching her hairline. "I mean, you know it was her first, right?"

I'm sort of stunned. "No. No way."

"Trust me, Aidan. I know." Her voice is deliberate and she's still staring.

I have no words. Kate was so forward and so confident that it never even crossed my mind.

"She didn't tell you?" Jen's voice has softened, but only a little. Her shoulders have also fallen, and I'm hoping this means she's not as pissed as she was a moment ago.

"No. She didn't tell me." My heart's starting to race. I'm trying to replay everything. Nothing she did or said made me feel like it was her first time. Nothing. Why didn't she tell me? I mean, I don't think I would have done anything different, except for maybe I would have gotten out of bed with her this morning and spent some time, or been more careful.... But shit, she told me to stay in bed. Well, actually, I probably would have stopped it. Probably. Maybe. I think about her shirt dropping to the floor. The curve of her body. I'm not sure if I would have stopped it or not.

Was I careful enough? Now I feel like shit for not asking.

I shake my head still a bit stunned. And it's a big deal because I should have known, but not a big deal because it doesn't matter that much. Mostly it's confusing the hell out of me that she didn't say anything.

"Do you know why she had salad last night instead of pizza?" Jen's voice is quiet as she stuffs her hands in her pockets.

My mouth's drying out. "Because she's a girl?"

Jen lets out a breath. "You two need to talk."

"That's what we did. Last night. We left when you had your tongue down Toby's throat, and we talked." I felt like we talked for half the night as we walked the neighborhood.

Jen still looks annoyed, but I don't think it's directed at me. "Sorry. I was mad 'cause you were in your room sleeping, and she was practically glowing. You should have been glowing together. And it should have been nauseating to watch."

A smile starts to spread even though it won't help me if Jen's still pissed. Because I've gotta admit, I feel a little proud of the fact Kate came out *glowing*.

"I just. Yeah." She's not looking at me anymore. She's looking confused. "When you see Kate, tell her you two need to talk."

I nod. Why wouldn't she tell me? Was she worried about what I'd think knowing she'd never done it before? And *she* undressed *me*. My head's spinning.

I turn around and decide to eat cold pizza for breakfast. Maybe

I'll head up to see the guys. I'll call Kate on my way, but first I need to figure out what to say.

❖

Okay. As soon as I start to dial her number in the car, I realize that this is not the kind of conversation I should be having on the phone. I need to go to Kate's house.

❖

Kate answers the door and her smile splits her face when our eyes meet.

"Hey." She leans forward and kisses my cheek.

"Bring him in!" A girl who must be Kate's sister waves from behind her—similar faces, same brown hair.

The house is smaller than I expected for Kate's dad to be a doctor. Foster's an accountant and lives in a practical mansion.

Okay. Meeting the parents. The day after having sex with their daughter. This should be…interesting.

I shake hands with her parents and the sister and the sister's husband, and it's all very bizarre and overwhelming and makes what Kate and I did last night make me feel like a bit of a stalker slime ball or something. All I can think over and over is *I had sex with your daughter. I had sex with your sister.* Over and over and over and over.

Lane, her sister's husband, obviously just got there because they're all in the living room asking him a million questions, and now asking me a million questions, only I'm not ready to answer any of them and I can feel my blood pressure rising, and all I want is to be in my car on the road to see the guys—even if being on post sounds like a shitty way to spend my day.

I lean into her slightly. "Kate. Can we talk for a sec?"

Our eyes meet and she smiles way too wide, and leans in way too close, for family company letting her lips touch my ear as she whispers back. "Yeah. Sure."

"I'm on my way up to Washington for couple of days." Will she take my leaving the wrong way?

"A couple days?" Her brows rise in surprise.

Her sister gives me a look that says she knows what happened last night and here I am talking about taking off for a few. Great. I'm in too deep here. *Way* too deep.

I nod and smile again at the parents before walking toward the front door.

Kate follows me back to the porch.

"My unit's back," I say as we step outside. "And the guys want me to come up."

"Oh."

"I wanted to see you before I left." I'm confused about her not sharing last night, so I don't know how my voice sounds.

"What's the matter?" She reaches out and touches my arm.

I need to say it. Ask her. "I talked with Jen this morning."

"Oh?" Her face looks fake—a fake smile. She's too still.

I lower my voice as low as I can. "She said that you'd never…"

Kate's cheeks immediately turn red.

"I didn't want you to make a big deal, or…" She's shaking her head and smiling like it isn't a big deal, only it is. I think.

"Don't. Kate." I step closer. "You should have told me."

Her face falls. "I'm sorry. I hate being treated differently."

And I can't help but understand that.

"Would you not have? I mean, would you have stopped us?" She's so close that the heat from her body starts to take over my thought process.

"I don't know, Kate. I don't even know how to answer that question because I shared all that stuff with you, and you didn't tell me something that seems like pretty important information for what we did last night." I can't believe how open I'm being with her now. The old Aidan would have driven away and let it lie. But now that seems wrong, or rude.

I'm facing her, though. That feels big. Significant. We're talking.

"Aidan. I'm sorry." She swallows once. And again. Her large brown eyes are so filled with worry.

I pull her into me before I think about it too much. She feels good here. My face rests against the side of her head. "I really need you to be honest with me, okay?"

"Okay. I promise."

"Anything else?" Jen said that we needed to talk, and I'm not sure if this covers it or not. Especially because she's not feeling as distracting as she normally does. Maybe because this is suddenly almost as complicated as everything else.

"Nope."

I rub my hand up and down her back a few times. "So, I'm headed out."

"Yeah. You said. Call me you know, if you want to, or…"

She feels bad, I can tell by the way her voice is quiet and the way she's not looking at me.

I smile because I don't want her to feel bad. She's starting to become more than the distraction I was looking for. "Of course I'll call you." Oh wait. I pull my phone out. "Picture?" I know this kind of stuff is a big deal to girls.

She grins. "Yeah."

We press our faces close like the pictures I make fun of, and I take the shot. As soon as I pull my arm down, I'm staring at her lips, and I'm not sure who started this, but we're pressed together. Our lips together. I almost forget we're on her parents' porch before I slow the kiss to something that won't get my ass chewed out by her dad.

I kiss her cheek twice more, even though I'm still feeling a bit confused about what she does share with me, and after talking to Jen, part of me wonders if there are other things I maybe should know.

"Gotta run." I step back.

"See you." She waves as I jog to my car.

I wave before shifting into drive, and grabbing the steering wheel.

Kate stands on her porch until I'm gone.

And I'm frustrated that this is so mixed. I mean, I think we're okay, but I realize that I've shared a ton of stuff with her that I didn't even intend to share, and she hasn't said much outside of surface conversation. Is that normal? Am I not worth it? Does she not trust me? I'm realizing that at this point she has a lot more reason to trust me than I have to trust her. I'm definitely in new territory here, and that's the last thing I need.

I'm outside of the company building sitting on a table in a covered park area with Butch and Roberts. They're on leave so no one's in uniform. It's almost like it used to be. I have no idea if this makes me miss it more or less.

I still have too much stuff floating around in my head. School. Army. Now Kate. Future. No arm. Melinda Pilot.

The questions from the guys have been near constant ranging from touching girls to unhooking bras to driving with one arm.

"You can't even light a fucking match!" Butch says as he sucks in another drag off his cigarette.

"Fuck you." I shake my head, grab a match and light it on the concrete, tossing it at him once it's lit.

"Go bother someone else." Roberts shoves him.

Butch does this openmouthed cackling laugh before walking away. He'll be back, and be as annoying as always.

"I hate that stupid fucker." Roberts flicks ash onto the pavement.

"Yeah. I only had to put up with him in close quarters for six months. Not a whole year."

"Not like you got out of it easy, Con." Roberts tosses his cigarette to the ground and grinds it out with his boot.

I can't believe we're actually talking about this. Like it's real, and not like we're joking about left-handed masturbation. "No. Not easy."

"Let's go up. I'm in my own room now."

"Right. *Sergeant.*" I give him a half-assed, left-handed salute before dropping my cigarette to the ground and stamping it out with my foot. I don't smoke often, but when everyone around you gets a five-minute smoke break, you pick up the habit.

It's weird being inside the company again. The painted tan, brick, hallways are the same. Stairs with chipping metal railings are the same. He's on the third floor now. Single enlisted rooms. It's almost like the one I shared with him before we left, only he's not sharing anymore.

"So, how are things really?" He kicks his door shut, and the guy has the same game posters and Pink Floyd wall-hanging when we roomed together. It's bizarre.

Only one bed in this room, though. But he's got a small couch, TV, mini-fridge. Moving up in the world.

"Con?"

"Shitty." That's really the best word, and the easiest explanation. There's way too much stuff to answer the question of how are things? I flop on his couch and he slouches on his bed.

"Girl?"

I pull up the picture of Kate and toss him my phone, glad I took it.

He catches it and his brows go up. "Damn, Connelly."

"She's too young." I shake my head. "And..." But I don't want to get deep. Not about her. It's too new and I'm still confused about where we're at with each other.

"But she's hot. And not just a little hot, but smokin' hot." He leans forward and hands my phone to me—something he'd never do if I still had both arms. He'd have thrown the damn thing as hard as he could.

I nod.

"You like her?" He runs a hand over his nearly shaved head, and I suddenly feel weird about how long I've let mine get.

I nod again and keep my mouth closed.

"Know what's next for you yet?"

"Nope."

He doesn't ask me anything else.

Roberts knows me well enough to know that I'm not ready to talk about any of this yet. I don't want to talk about my life right now. My future. None of it.

"Tell me about the rest of the tour," I say.

"Fucking lame-ass word. Tour." He slumps against the wall. "Makes it sound like a damn vacation and it sure as shit wasn't."

I can't agree with that more.

He tells me about the guys, and a girl he ran into who's stationed at Bragg. She's supposed to be home from Afghanistan in a month and he's going to go out and visit her. We talk half the night about nothing important, drink a few beers, and at some point in time I fall asleep on the tiny futon. He doesn't offer me the bed. We would have fought over it if I had both arms, and he knows damn well that offering the thing to me would be an insult.

Mostly I wonder if coming up here counts as checking something off my list, even though I know I didn't talk about all the shit that Foster would have wanted me to.

Maybe next time.

17

Kate Walker

The world feels different in a million ways. First off, I used to feel like the last virgin in my senior class, aside from maybe Jen. Now I feel a bit…in the minority. I'm mixed on this one, but I'm okay with this because of Aidan and because the whole thing…Foreign. Familiar. Mostly him. His chest. His abs. The way his arm wrapped around me, and the feel of him sleeping behind me…

Okay. I'm distracted.

Second, Aidan left for a couple days the day after we had sex. Do I read into that? Do I not read into that? I'm hoping this is simply my neurotic self, thinking too much.

Deena's given me this bizarre lecture a million times about it's not that I had sex, it's that I just jumped into bed with some random guy. But Aidan's not random, and he's also not just some guy. He gets life-changing situations. He gets how crappy and bizarre and uncertain your future is when you're facing something you never expected to face. Also. Deena's the one who kept saying I liked him. That, right there takes him off the "random" list. If there is such a thing.

All of these things are reasons that when Aidan gets home I'll talk to him about my diabetes. The sucky thing is that he said, *please be honest with me*. And I froze up, and now, just like Jen and Deena said, what shouldn't be a big deal, has the chance of being a big deal.

Deena and Lane are using my room, and I don't even want to know if that's what they're doing in there.

No matter what, I plan on giving them space until one or both of them emerges. For now I'm parked on the couch with Mom and Dad in front of the TV, watching…I don't even know what, but there are houses involved.

"About college." Dad's voice is way too careful for a casual conversation.

"Yes?" My heart's already hammering. I don't want to talk about college. I want to hang with Aidan. He's been gone a day, and I want to be back in his arms, back in his bed, the world shut outside. Even just watching the lame program about houses would be better. Instead I'm about to get bad news. I can tell.

"With your health," Mom continues. "I know you wanted to go farther away, but I think that for a year or two, it would be best to stick closer to home."

"What?" This only came up when I was first diagnosed, and Mom was all worried about every single part of my future. Husband, kids, school, and I could tell that all she wanted was for me to be close. Preferably within sight or sound for every moment of my day. I thought we were past that. "Jen and I have plans. It's all arranged."

Dad scoots forward in his chair. "I know you really wanted to go to California, and I know there are good doctors there, but Kate, I don't think you've had more than two weeks where you didn't bottom out or have blood sugar so high that any normal person would have serious issues."

"You can't stop me. I'll be eighteen." Oooh. That was *not* a smart thing to say. That wouldn't have even be a smart thing to *think*.

Dad's jaw tightens before he speaks. "But I can refuse to pay for it."

I'm about to jump up and scream or something. How can this be happening? Jen and I are supposed to go to school together in the fall. USC. Beaches. Warm weather.

"Kate." Mom's voice is the calm one this time. "I'm so scared for you. I'm scared about your health, and the fact that you don't seem bothered is what has us most worried. I'm telling you that you need to make sure you're ready to go to college here in the fall if you need to. If between now and when you have to give your final word to USC, you're able to manage your diabetes, your father and I will support you."

Dad's whole body is tense, and I get the feeling that he wants me here for at least another year no matter what.

"I can't believe you're doing this." I stand up. "I've had diabetes for a year. At any point in time you could have said that—"

"No, no, no." Dad stands. "We warned you as soon as it was obvious that you weren't taking your disease seriously that there would be major consequences including when and where you went to college."

"I don't believe this." I move toward the hallway.

"We're not done, Kate," Dad says.

"We're done for now." I don't want to ask what I need to do to go away because I don't want to know. I don't want to do it. I want out.

When will Aidan be back?

As I near my room I remember Deena and Lane are in there. Perfect.

"I want you to be excited, Lane." Deena's voice sounds pleading.

"How am I supposed to be excited, Deena? Timing really couldn't be worse. On top of that, it's kind of embarrassing that you're pregnant right after we got married. Like we're one of those weird people who doesn't believe in sex before marriage or birth control."

I want to slap that man. This is a side of Lane that I've definitely never seen before.

"You're embarrassed of me?" And there's the agitation that Deena's voice should have. At least she's not throwing up every minute any more.

"No." His voice softens. "It's the situation. It's just…"

"Can we talk about something else? *Please?* I can't keep having this conversation with you." I know my sister well enough to know her irritation has turned to tears. "I'm pregnant. The baby is coming."

"I know. It's that I—"

"Just go. Please," she pleads.

There's silence between them and then my bedroom door opens to Lane who gives me a quick nod before heading to the living room.

I run into my room and pull my sister into my arms. "I'm sorry," I whisper. "I didn't realize you two were arguing like this."

"I'm going to throw up." She pushes away from me and runs for the bathroom.

Right now I don't even know which is worse. My situation or hers. I flop on the bed without a solution to either.

Jen, Deena and I are on a girl movie binge. No word from Aidan, but I keep flipping the phone over and over in my hands.

"Call him," Jen says. "You guys need to talk anyway, because you need to tell him—"

"No." I shake my head. "I…" I'm not sure if I'm ready to talk to him about my stupid disease.

She rolls her eyes. "Please."

"Kate. You slept with him. If you want to call. *Call.*" Deena's eyes are wide.

"I don't want to call," I insist. *I want him to call me.* But he hasn't. He's probably busy. And anyway. I was the one who lied to him about my experience. Or, at least, didn't tell him the whole truth. He seemed upset, which makes it scarier to call because I feel like I definitely screwed up a bit. It makes telling him about my diabetes not only something I don't want to do, but a little scary because I'm not sure how he'll react.

"You're just being stubborn!" Deena leans forward. I haven't seen her this animated since she got here.

"Can we leave it? I'm still in shock over Mom and Dad wanting me to stay here for college." I'm mad about the whole thing. What's the good of turning eighteen if my parents are still going to control everything I do?

"What if you agreed to the insulin pump?" Jen asks.

"What?" That came out of nowhere.

"You know how they're always on about that. What if you said you'd do the insulin pump. Do you think you could come with me then?" Her wide blue eyes look almost pleading.

The thought of her going off to college without me sucks, but an insulin pump…

"I dunno," I mumble. I can't imagine having one of those. How awkward would it have made it to be with Aidan? Some electronic thing strapped to me. A small tube inserted in my skin. I shudder at how weird and gross that would be. *Attached.*

"I don't think I can do it," I say.

Jen sighs. Deena sighs.

"Okay, seriously." I stand up. "Mom and Dad have already given me grief today. Can we finish the movie?"

I want to scream that I'm done talking about Aidan.

I'm done talking about diabetes.

I'm done talking about college.

I'm done talking to them.

Everyone's faces turn pointedly toward the screen, but I'm not sure how much any of us sees. They're supposed to be helping, and instead they're making my life more stressful.

18

AIDAN CONNELLY

I get the familiar looks from people on base—a mix of sympathy and knowing. They all know what happened to me—or their own version of it. A guy on a military base with a missing limb isn't exactly a mystery. Instead of feeling their stares, I keep glancing at my phone wondering if I should drop Kate a text, or call her or if I should wait to hear from her.

"What's with you and your phone?" Roberts elbows me as we walk through the commissary to stock up his snack bin and mini-fridge.

"Oh. Nothing." Wondering what to say to Kate with how awkward things were when we left. On the surface, it was okay. But underneath, where everything confusing in my life lives, that's where Kate and I got all mixed up. One simple thing. Well, two. Sex, and her not telling me something I should have known before the sex.

For the first time, I don't want to use the word *sex*, but a guy like me doesn't say *make love*. But what do I call it when it feels like the way it did with her? Like I couldn't get enough of her body, but also like I was glad she stayed the night. That I didn't have to let her go.

"Connelly?" Roberts is laughing as he waves his hand in front of my face.

I hit his arm away, but my phone flies from my hand and smashes on the floor.

"Shit." Roberts looks back at the pieces.

We stare at each other, knowing that if I had both arms, I'd have been able to hold my phone in one hand, and smack him away with the other.

"My own damn fault." I try to laugh, but we both get it. And the weight of the little ways my life has changed hit me hard. Again.

"Call the girl. Use mine." He shoves his phone at me as he picks up the pieces of mine.

"I don't know her number. It was in my phone."

Roberts starts to hand me the pieces, but I have his cell in my hand, and can't take mine back. The whole damn situation sucks. I shove his phone in my pocket and start to take the pieces of mine. It's not as bad as I would have thought.

"I'll get it." Roberts slides the battery back in, but the back is shattered. He pushes the power button, and the thing miraculously turns on.

"Thanks," I mumble as I hand him his phone and then take mine. Single steps. One thing at a time. "I should get going."

There's an odd pause between us as the reality of how different we are settles in.

"That's it? You're not going to stick around?"

I want out. I don't care that Kate got a little confusing. A little confusing is better than the shitty feeling that comes from being around the kind of guy I used to be.

"Con, wait." Roberts walks up behind me.

I didn't even totally realize that I was walking away. "I'll call ya." And I walk out. Walk the mile around the airfield, back to the company building, and back to my car.

I drive away from the Army base that should be my home.

I pass the exit that would take me to Pilot's wife. For more than an hour, nothing reminds me of anything.

I pass the community college.

I pass my shrink's offices.

I drive by Mom's exit.

It's already dark, but I wonder if I should drop by and see Kate. I call her and hit the speaker button. It's the only way I can talk and drive.

Kate answers on the first ring. "Hey."

"Hey. I missed you." Already I'm over the line of casual.

"Me too. I would've called, but I didn't know how mad you were, and I didn't want to interrupt."

"Can I stop by?"

The pause is too long.

Shit. I shouldn't have asked.

"My parents are going on about college and talking with my sister and me tonight. I'd love to, but I can't."

Now I need to sound normal. Not too disappointed. "Okay. I mean. That's fine."

"Tomorrow?"

"Pick you up after school?" Now I'm way too eager. And parents and school and *what the hell am I doing?*

"I'm sorry. You're going to think I'm not worth the trouble, but I can't do right after school either."

I'm a jerk, but I do wonder if she's worth the trouble, but no way will I tell her. And worth the trouble isn't how I'd put it either because it's really that I'm in a bad position to be what she deserves. And it sucks to be sort of dating someone who has to ask her parents to go out. Should I be doing this? Or maybe I don't care if I should be or not, because despite the occasional difficulty, I really want to.

"How about tomorrow night? Is that cool?"

"Yeah. Call me then."

We hang up, but it all feels awkward and stilted, and I don't know if that's normal or not. Maybe because we were *together*, together, and then had that thing she didn't tell me, and then I was gone. Maybe it's the whole parents thing.

Right now I hope I can sleep, and I hope that when we're together tomorrow it feels as good as I remember.

19

Kate Walker

I'm at school late waiting for Jen, and about to head home to get ready for my date with Aidan tonight. It's been an odd few days without him. At the same time, I know we have to talk when I see him again, so it's also been a strange kind of relief.

A girl's sniffing around the corner. Not I-have-a-cold sniffing, *crying* sniffing.

"Tamara, he's a jerk, okay?" A girl's voice comes through the hallway, but I can't see her yet. "You can do so much better."

Tamara? Better than Shelton? Right. She's just a girl who looks good in a cheerleading uniform.

Wow, I'm a snob.

And he broke up with her? That makes no sense. He's not the kind of guy to use someone for...whatever he and Tamara had. But it felt like he broke up with me to be with her, so I would've thought they'd last a bit longer.

More sniffing and quiet voices.

I know this is one of those situations where I need to turn around and walk away, but I don't. I stop my feet; I stop my breathing, and wish that I could stop my heart on the off chance it might be beating loud enough for them to hear.

"You guys only went on a few dates," a girl says.

"I know, but...I never thought I could be with someone like him, you know? Smart. Sweet. I'm just..."

"Come on, let's go get some ice cream or something, okay?"

There's this whiny-like, "Umm-hmm." And now, again, is when I need to turn and move. Or run. But instead I stand like an idiot, staring at the corner as they come around.

"Oh." Tamara wipes her face with her cheer sweatshirt. "Perfect."

"Well, he broke up with me too." I shrug, amazed that I have something to say to Tamara. Here are my ugly snobby thoughts again.

She looks at me all wary-like as her friend leads her away.

I was just trying to be *nice*. Guess I shouldn't be surprised. I'm one of the girls who roll her eyes every day they wear their cute little uniforms.

Still. Shelton breaking up with her is bizarre.

I follow Jen out to her car, and I start to reach out to open the door when I remember I'm trying to go one-armed. Just to test it out. I use my other arm, but it means my pack falls off my shoulder.

"Crap," I mutter.

"What are you *doing*?" Jen's brows go up as she gives me this odd smile.

"One arm," I explain, as I jerk open the car door. But when I get in, I have to find a spot for my pack before I can even think about pulling my seatbelt across my lap or closing my door. It all takes a couple minutes. Just to get in.

"How's it going there?" she teases as she starts her car. She's buckled, lip-glossed and her bag is tucked in the back seat.

"This really sucks!" I start to laugh, but also feel this little pang of sadness for him. Even the everyday stuff is a pain.

"Are you doing this just so you have an excuse to stick a needle in his stomach when you tell him you're diabetic?" she asks.

"Hmm. I hadn't thought of that." I start to laugh, but the tragedy of his accident sort of hits me again. "They're not really comparable, and besides, I bet he's had a lot of needles stuck in him since he got hurt."

Jen puts the car in drive. The silence between us feels a bit heavy and sad. I've been really stupid not to tell him. We'd understand each other better—or maybe he'd just see that I understand him a little more than most people. What a hypocrite I've been—if that's the right word. Being all open about his problem, and so closed off about mine.

"You okay?" Jen asks.

"I'm going to talk to him tonight." I say it with determination, even though this subtle shaking starts in my core, and I'm already wondering how much harder I'll be shaking by tonight.

"It'll be fine." She gives me her best reassuring smile. "Just tell him why you didn't. I think he'll understand."

I slump in the passenger's seat, and barely remember I can't cross my arms, 'cause I'm pretending to only have one. "I hope so."

Let me just say that it's a good thing Aidan's not a girl, because makeup and a straightener? Not easy with only one hand. I poke my eye twice with my eyeliner pencil, and now my eye is all red. I give up after burning my ear and temple with the straightener. At least I tried—that has to be worth something. But now that Aidan will be here any minute, I'm more than just freaking out over talking to him. The shaking is definitely worse.

I draw in a deep breath and take a minute to calculate out the carbs in the Subway he said he packed. I allow myself the use of both hands while I do my shot in the bathroom, and I'm glad I thought of doing this before we get together so I don't have to excuse myself to go to the bathroom later. Though, I'm telling him. I totally am. So even if I hadn't done this now, it would still be okay. Hopefully.

I stare in the mirror after I put my pharmacy away, knowing he's on his way here. If I'd known we were going to get so close, I probably would have told him the night we met. I just didn't expect to like him so much.

"Okay. You can do this. Easy." I raise my brows and give myself a look like my mom would give me. Then I sigh. I'm just not feeling the confidence I want to.

Wait. I focus on the mirror again, and put on what I think is a sweet, sympathetic face, but instead I look constipated.

I'm crap at this. Whatever. *Just say it.*

"I know I should have said something sooner, but it was nice having someone who didn't know this about me, because it feels like my family and friends treat me different." It sounds so contrived, and I still look constipated. Ugh. I suck. I spin away from the mirror disgusted when I hear a knock at the door.

My heart jumps, and my stomach flips over. Then I realize that if I don't get the door, *Dad* will get the door.

"Don't stay out too late," Dad says as I run up the hallway and grab the bag with snacks waiting on the floor.

"I won't." I slow as I try to step past him in the living room.

I reach for the door, but Dad leans back and gets it first. No doubt wanting to check Aidan out again. Curse this small house.

"Hello, Dr. Walker." Aidan stretches his hand out, looking a lot more sure of himself than he did when he came by a few days ago.

His smile is pretty awesome—even when it isn't directed at me.

"Nice to see you again, Aidan. It's a school night, so not past nine or so. Maybe ten if I get a phone call." Dad's voice is friendly enough, but it's just going to be another reminder for Aidan how young I am. I've already not been able to see him for the last day and a half because of my parents.

"No problem." Aidan's eyes wander to mine briefly, and then meet Dad's again.

"See you soon, sweetie." Dad kisses my head, and I roll my eyes, which gets a grin from Aidan.

"Finally." I breathe out as Dad closes the door.

"Ready?" he asks.

"Very."

Aidan's arm comes around me, and it's like my body folds into his. Into his warmth. Into the way he feels against me.

"Glad to see you." He smiles wide and gives me a soft kiss.

"You too." And as I pull slowly away from his arm, and his eyes hit mine, I know I'll tell him. Just not right now. Later. But tonight. Almost for-sure definitely.

20

AIDAN CONNELLY

Kate's been quiet on the whole drive, and fidgety. Neither is like her.

"What's up?" I ask, wondering if I want to know.

"Do you ever wish you could hide the loss of your arm?" she asks.

I open my mouth, but I'm not sure how to answer. It makes me realize that already, it's sort of become part of who I am. I mean, I'd like to have my arm back, but would I try to hide the fact that it's missing? I don't think so. Not anymore. Especially not if she's going to touch my scars like she did last time we were together.

She pulls in a deep breath. "There's this thing I've needed to tell you about."

With how weird she's being I'm starting to feel like I can't breathe, like something might really be wrong between us. After my couple days with Roberts, I really want my night with Kate to go right. "You still like me?" I try to tease.

"Of course." Her smile is wide, and her cheeks pink, allowing me to take a breath in. This girl has really gotten to me, and I like it way more than I thought I would.

"We're okay then. I'm gonna pay for parking, and we'll take our food down to the beach, okay?" I stand out of the car into the blissfully empty parking lot—grateful not everyone is as brave about low clouds as we are.

"Okay." She stands up, and holds the doorframe with white knuckles.

I watch her for a sec. "You okay?"

"Just dizzy." She rolls her eyes. "It's nothing." Her voice is so quiet.

"Okay." I jog toward the pay slots. I can't believe I'm going on a picnic, outside, with a girl. It's seriously something straight out of a movie. But I'm looking forward to it—hanging with Kate. I fill out the envelope, and stuff the money in.

When I turn around, Kate's sitting on the hood, looking very pale. I start to jog back.

She turns, and blinks a few times. Her mouth opens, but she just makes this weird humming sound.

My heart starts to pound. "Kate?" Something is definitely weird here.

"I shot. Was in a hurry at home." She sounds drunk, slurred. "Too long. No food." She pulls in this deep breath as her eyes fill with fear.

I sprint, but she's still on the opposite side of the car.

Her mouth opens a few times before she pushes out a word.

"Help."

I grab her just as her knees buckle against my legs.

"Shit, shit. Kate." My whole body's shaking. She went from dizzy to this in just a few minutes?

I have her under one arm, but I'm only holding her up because she's pressed into my side. *What the hell just happened?* I'm trying to walk, and she's trying to walk the three steps back to the car door, but her legs keep buckling, and each time they do, she slides farther down my side, and I'm losing my grip.

I can't lose my grip.

"I…ospital…sho-ot…foo…" Her voice sounds like she's talking through syrup. Sinking dread hits me in another wave. I don't know what to do. What's *wrong* with her?

"Can you grab me? At all?" Oh, shit. *I'm not going to be able to do this with one hand.* My head is nothing but fuzz. There's no thinking. Just anger and frustration. I *have* to do this faster. Get her in the car faster. I scan the parking lot, which was awesomely empty a few moments ago. Now I'm pissed that a few clouds are keeping people away.

Her fingers feebly pinch my shirt as she pushes into me, trying to help me hold on.

"What's happening, Kate? *What do I do?*"

She's trying to form words, but nothing's coming out right.

We're to the door, but I don't know how to get her in. She's a near rag-doll right now. I lean her against the car, using my body against hers to keep her from falling over, and pull open the door.

If she hits the ground, I'm not sure if I could lift her with one arm. She slumps farther just as I get my arm back around her. "Kate. *Kate!*"

Each second pushes me further and further into frantic mode. I know I need to call 911, but I can't let go of her.

I use my leg and my arm together, trying to balance her body. I need my other damn arm! I need to call 911!

"Fuck!"

I manage to slide her in the seat, using my arm, my leg, and my body, even though I'm shaking. She helps only slightly, and now she's in, but limp, and just blinking a bit, like she's fighting to keep her eyes open. I push her leg inside with my foot before closing the door, pulling out my phone, dialing 911. Now I have to set the damn thing on speaker so I can drive and talk. I'm shaking. This is like the nightmares; I can't help, only *way* too real. I leap in the car and tear out of the parking lot. We're headed back to town at about ninety when 911 answers. Kate's breathing, but almost completely unresponsive. Her eyes half blink a few more times. I can't lose her. *Can't.*

"Nine-one-one. Please state your emergency." A woman's voice answers.

"My girlfriend passed out. I don't know why. I'm in the car. She said something about a shot. I think." Kate. Shot? My heart's pounding so hard I'm worried I won't be able to hear the woman at the other end.

"Is she using drugs?"

"No!" I yell.

"Are you sure?"

"I—" Shit. I don't know anything. *"Just help her!"*

"I need you to pull over until an ambulance can get to you."

Fuck that. "I'm ten minutes away, tops." My foot's hard on the floor. Kate's eyelids are still twitching.

"I need you to check for a pulse. Is she still breathing?"

Holy shit this is all too real. "She's breathing." I can't believe I'm saying these words.

"Can you check her wrists for a bracelet or a necklace that might indicate a medical condition?"

"What?" No. I can't. "I only have one arm and I'm using it to drive." Tears are streaming down my face, and I've never been more frantic and angry about my handicap than I am now. I jerk on the steering wheel a few times. "Shit!"

"I need you to calm down." This woman's calm voice is pissing me off. "I need you to pull off the side of the road. We'll find you."

"I'm not stopping the damn car!"

"Do you have her full name and date of birth?" The woman's voice stays calm.

"Kate Walker, and...*fuck, I don't know!*"

"I need you to breathe, okay? Where are you now?"

"Five minutes away, tops." But I still can't control my breathing. I don't even care about crying. *I just need my other arm.* I want to touch her. Touch her hair. Her arm. Feel her breathe. Check for some bracelet or something.

Can't be, though. She can't have some medical condition. Kate would have said something.

Would she? Maybe she was just using you, Aidan. You know this started out as you using her for distraction.

No! But I'm shaking. Right now anything and everything feels possible.

"I've warned the hospital you're coming," the woman says.

"*What do I do?*" I'm now weaving through traffic, and the hospital's in sight. I keep glancing over at Kate, but I'm afraid to steer with my knee to touch her when I'm driving this fast.

As I screech to a stop in front of the ER, they're waiting for me. Two guys, both with *two* arms, pull her out, set her on a bed, and run her inside. I want to go in with her, but I'm yelled at to move my car so I jump in, my body tensed and shaking.

I dial Jen on my way inside and try to tell her what happened, but my voice keeps quivering as the shock of the situation this me again and again.

"Kate's really bad about staying on top of it," Jen says. "I'll call her parents."

"On top of what?" I yell.

Silence.

"Dammit, Jen! I've just had one of the shittiest experiences of my life. What the fuck is going on!"

"She's diabetic. Takes shots. All of it. If she passed out, maybe she did her shot at home guessing what you guys were going to eat, and messed it up. She's not very good at—"

I hang up. Numbness sweeps through me just before disbelief, and then my insides shatter.

The nurse comes out and asks me a million questions I can't answer. When did Kate last have a shot? When did she eat? Do I have any information that'll help? All I get to do is relive watching her face go slack, her voice get funny, and the weight of her in my arms, and me feeling desperate to help her, having no idea how to do it with only one arm.

My body's heavy, exhausted, filled with disbelief.

"When can I see her?" I ask the nurse, half ready to bolt around her and start checking rooms.

"Are you family?" The nurse looks over her glasses.

"I, no, but I brought her in." That's got to count for *something*.

"Sorry. Family only." She shakes her head and turns away. "You can have a seat and wait."

Wait.

Wait.

I still can't stop the damn tears. Kate's so close. *So close.* But I can't talk to anyone. Can't see her. Can't touch her.

And how the hell did she think it was okay not to tell me this?

She has to do *shots*. It's not something that slipped her mind. It's something she kept from me. Had to *plan* to keep from me.

I stare at a fake fire in the waiting room for what feels like an eternity.

Kate's parents come in, and I jog toward them, hoping for answers.

Her dad puts his arm around me. "She'll be fine. Come on."

I barely know the guy, but he's about to get me in to maybe see her, or to at least know what's going on. "Thanks."

"Aidan. Thank you. You have no idea." His voice shakes, and his hand pats my back once before letting me go.

We're ushered to a waiting room where I'm pelted with the same questions from her father as I got from the nurse. He explains that she took her insulin before leaving the house, and then when she didn't eat soon enough, her blood sugar dropped. Like Jen guessed. He's been on the phone with the doctor at the hospital and Kate will be fine. Her low isn't as dangerous as a high, but is still a big deal. All I can think is how she hid this from me. How I could've talked with her. I'd understand probably better than most people she knows, and she didn't trust me with it. It doesn't make sense.

Her dad stands up and talks quietly with a doctor then disappears into Kate's room at the end of the hall.

Deena sits next to me. She puts her hand on my good shoulder and speaks barely above a whisper.

I'm still trying not to shake.

She tells me about Kate getting her diagnosis, and how she's fought against it every step of the way. But Kate's version of fighting is trying to ignore it, which has landed her in the ER more than once. Deena tells me about how Kate might be stuck here next year, and how her parents want her on an insulin pump. Why she should do it, and why she hates the idea so much.

"You can tell Kate I told you everything," Deena says quietly. "I've never seen her fall for someone the way she's fallen for you."

I'm not sure if I'm happy about that, or if it makes me angrier.

"Thanks. For telling me, I mean." I try a smile that I know completely fails.

"Sorry she's so stubborn." The corner of Deena's mouth twitches in a partial smile.

I nod again because I'm still sort of in shock. I'm in the hospital. For Kate.

Her dad waves her mom inside. I'm still waiting with Deena, but now we sit in silence. I don't have anything to say. Maybe one thing. "I like your sister way more than I expected to."

Deena chuckles. "Kate's funny that way."

Funny. And now I'm starting to wonder—what the hell is she doing with me? A one-armed guy who has no idea what to do with his life, a crazy family life, and a past he doesn't want to face.

At the same time—what the hell am I doing with her? She only tells me half-truths, and is just too young to be involved with someone who has my issues. Well, and she obviously doesn't care about me knowing her.

I'm weak now. The adrenaline's gone, and exhaustion is taking over. Kate's mom steps out of her room, making eye contact with me, and holding the door open so I can step in.

No one speaks.

Maybe I look that pissed. Maybe I'm more afraid than I want to be and they can see it on my face. It doesn't matter why we're quiet.

Her dad steps out. Her mom gives me a weak smile.

I leap out of my chair and go into Kate's room.

Kate's in a hospital gown with an IV in her arm, and dark circles under her eyes. I want to cry, and punch my fist through something, and scream. But I stand at the foot of her bed. Still. And wait for her to talk.

21
Kate Walker

Aidan's face is pale. And he's too still.

This is definitely not a good way for him to learn about my diabetes. I'm re-playing all the millions of times that I could have said something and didn't. How much I like him, am starting to *more* than like him, and how I screwed this up so badly. I have to lighten this. Make him see that it's not a huge deal.

"I know this is all very dramatic and whatever…" I roll my eyes.

"Don't," he says as his jaw clenches and his head starts to shake.

His breathing fills the room, and I'm terrified of what he's going to say next.

"Don't joke about this. I was scared as hell, Kate. I didn't know what to do. It took everything I had to get you in my car." He rubs his hand down his face, and I swear his chin pulls like mine does just before I cry.

He can't cry. Aidan crying would be worse than either of my parents.

I'm so *stupid*. "I was pretty out of it," I whisper. He did so well. I mean, I sort of remember him helping me into his car, and some yelling on the phone…

He does this way-too-slow breathe in. And then a breathe out. I know that if this were my dad, it would be a huge deal. "I don't even mind that, Kate. If it helped you, I'd learn all about your diabetes, and what you needed or whatever. But you never gave me the chance. Hell, I might have known what better to do. Stick a candy in your mouth or made sure you got your food or something, but you never said anything."

"I asked you this earlier. Wouldn't you hide the loss of your arm if you could?"

"No!" He throws his arm in the air. "I wouldn't. Because like it or not, it's part of who I am now, just like whether you like it or not, being diabetic is part of who you are. And it's something you should've trusted me with."

I'm frantic now, but I'm stuck here with a needle in my arm. "I'm sorry. I'm sorry for passing out on you like that, and—"

"Don't you get it? It's not about you *passing out*. You know me, Kate! And you never gave me the chance to know you!" Once again his breathing fills the room, and my heart starts to break at the knowledge that I made him feel this way.

I want him to know me. I just want him to like what he sees. There's already so many annoying things—my blurts of honesty, my age, the fact that I still have to ask my parents if we want to go out…Maybe I was afraid that the diabetes would be too much.

"But I trust you, Aidan. I trusted that you could take care of me, and you got me here." I'm trying to smile, but his scared, pale face is scaring me. Making my heart flutter, and my chest tight.

"Kate. That's insane. You could have gone into a coma or something in the car. It was luck that got us here on time! And you *don't* trust me or you would have said something forever ago!"

My chest sinks further. No, no. "But I—"

"No! I know plenty of people who are disfigured, hurt, killed, and you, by not doing everything you can to keep yourself healthy, are going to end up the same way. And when you're ready to handle this for real, and take care of yourself, *then* we'll talk about trust, but I can't be around someone who lies to me and doesn't care enough about themselves to stay on top of a disease like this." His face has gone hard, and my heart's starting to break. "You have a choice."

"I'm so sorry." My cheeks are wet, and I'm trying to smear my tears away, but there are too many. "I just don't want this. It's like if I can ignore it, or set it aside—"

"Deal with it! You're in a fucking hospital. And from what I've learned from your sister, if you keep this up, this not maintaining or whatever, it could *kill you.*"

His eyes are hard on me.

I swallow a few times, trying to find the words to tell him that I *want* him to know me. Want him to be with me. Wish that he'd forgive me.

"Look around, Kate. You don't need to be here." His voice has turned this eerie fake calm. "I know plenty of people who died in circumstances out of their control. You're making yourself a victim when you don't need to."

I have to downplay. He's thinking it's more serious than it is. "It's not that dramatic, Aidan. I—"

"Grow up! It *is* that dramatic!" He turns toward the door. Away from me.

"Where are you going?" My voice barely works. He can't leave. Not like this.

"Do you care? It seems like this," he waves his arm between us, still not looking at me, "is something that would have made you and me closer. Showed that you wanted me to understand you, the way I felt you understood me. But you didn't."

"I do." I'm not even trying to wipe my tears anymore.

"I'll see you, Kate." He glances over at me for the briefest moment before walking out of my room.

I lie back in bed and my body starts to shake in sobs. There's shuffling, and people moving in or out, but I can't see, don't care.

Aidan's words hit hard. I didn't want this life so I didn't see how stupid I was being. I didn't take anything as seriously as I should have. I could go blind. I could die. *Die.*

How did I not get how serious my diabetes is until now?

Aidan was right about a lot of things. How stupid I'm being is probably the most important.

It's like all the pieces of my diabetes were strewn about in my mind, and now they've formed this diabetic house or something. This place that belongs to me whether I want it to or not, but it doesn't have to be a run-down old shack, it can be whatever kind of house I make it. Mine needs to be simple. And clean. And well taken care of.

I'm not even making sense to myself.

Deena climbs into bed with me. "I can't believe how he talked to you. I bet the whole hospital could hear."

Dad swallows and stares at the ceiling, blinking like he's trying not to cry, but his jaw is also clenched in anger. Maybe it's a good thing Aidan didn't stick around.

"He was right." I choke on the words as they come up. "I didn't want it to feel that way, but he's right."

Dad's eyes meet mine, and they look hopeful. Worried, like almost always, but hopeful.

"I'm so sorry. I didn't get it. I mean, I sort of got it, but not really. Not the way I should have." I wipe more tears.

Dad's legs buckle and he drops to sitting.

"I need to find people my age, you know, who have this too. And maybe if you think it would be good, I could try the insulin pump. For a while." Tears still pour down my face, but I can't stop them, and I'm afraid I'll start sobbing if I try, so I let them flow, and keep using my wet palms to wipe my cheeks.

Dad blinks a few times and tears escape. Mom's hands squeeze my feet and she's doing the weird chin frowny thing she does when we see the doctor, only I don't mind it as much as I used to.

"Proud of you, sis."

I lean against Deena and close my eyes, feeling completely drained.

My sister rolls onto her back. "Oh!" she squeals clutching her stomach.

"What?" I turn to face her.

"The baby moved!" Her eyes are as big as her smile.

"Really?" It hits me. My sister is having a baby. My sister. *A baby!*

"I'm going to be an aunt." I grin.

"Yeah, stupid." She giggles—*so Deena*—and it's this little bit of something really happy, and really kind of normal, but amazing, that pulls the room back into focus.

"Wow." I rest my hands on top of hers, which still clutch her stomach.

How did I not understand my diabetes, my sister's baby...I have this family who's all in here with me. Worried about me.

And for the first time since I was diagnosed, I think maybe, one day, I might be okay with it—with this little diabetic house I've built in my brain. I'm going to have to think about a way to make Aidan understand. It feels like I have to.

"Quite a group in here." The blond woman doctor who's been checking on me steps into the room.

All eyes are on her.

"We're going to watch you for another hour or two, and if you're still stable, we'll let you go home." She smiles. "I know you've wanted to go home since getting here."

"Yep." I sit up a little, more shaky from emotion than anything else.

"Are you sure?" Dad asks the doctor. A breath out—an uncertain one.

"You're a doctor." She turns toward Dad. "Keep her within sight or sound for twenty-four hours or so. She's fine."

"Not thirty-six?"

I hold back my eye roll and Deena chuckles next to me. "Let him negotiate," she whispers.

"I was being pretty conservative with twenty-four hours." The doctor winks at me. "And Dr. Masen said he'd like to see her in the office sometime over the next week. And maybe..." Her eyes float back to me. "I'll see you there, Kate."

"Thank you." I'm so ready to be out of this horrible gown and away from the memory of Aidan yelling at me in this room.

So, one part of my life is slowly being built. This diabetic part. Really, put together for the first time, since I never really did or thought about my disease the way I should have a long time ago. The other part, the part with Aidan that was my perfect escape, and the part that I thought was going so well...that I'm going to have to try to put together again. Somehow. As soon as my house arrest is over.

22

AIDAN CONNELLY

Everything about the situation is fucked up.

I care about her enough that I was terrified and angry I couldn't help. She was just supposed to be a distraction. How did she get to be so much more?

I can't believe how I yelled at her, but she sat there in a hospital gown, with a needle in her arm, and tried to blow it off.

And then all the shit that scares me about only having one arm—not being able to do the really important stuff—that was thrown back in my face with her near pass out. I can't take care of someone else. I won't be able to do anything when it really counts. There may be a million things I can do, but there are a million more things I can't.

I pull off the highway and end up in Pilot's neighborhood, but drive through knowing I'm too chickenshit to stop. Again.

Something's gotta give here, because I'm pretty sure I'm about to explode.

�

I'm on my back, on the mat, completely at the mercy of Bradley, his huge muscled arms trying to keep my useless shoulder from completely seizing up. I'm now wondering how long I'll have to keep coming in to see this guy. I probably don't want to know.

"So, Aidan. How's things?"

"That's a loaded question." I wince as his hands push my shoulder blade to the mat.

"Why's that?" he asks and he presses down on my chest and pulls up on the outer part of my shoulder.

"Because I'm pretty sure it all just blew to hell."

He chuckles. "Well, the good thing about times like that is you know it ain't gonna get any worse. Just better."

"I don't know. I thought that this morning."

"And then it got worse?" he asks.

I don't speak.

"You seeing your shrink?" Bradley smirks. He knows how much I hate that guy.

"I walked out early last time and haven't gone back."

"You feel better or worse?"

"Better about not seeing him, worse because life got messed up again."

"What's different?" He motions for me to flip to my stomach and I do.

Suddenly I find myself telling him about Kate, and then about meeting up with Roberts, and how we didn't argue about where to sleep, and how he had to put my phone back together for me. How I walked away. How I keep driving through Melinda's neighborhood without stopping in.

"You know what you need, Aidan?" Both his hands push down on my back and some of the tension in my shoulder actually loosens up.

"For you to climb off me?" I tease.

"A list." He sits back. "You can sit. Take a break."

I sit up and shift my head a few times because everything from my shoulders up feels weird when he's done with me. "I have a list."

"How far down the list are you?" He pulls his knees up and looks completely comfortable, like we're just going to hang in here for a while.

I tense at how presumptuous it is, but then lean back on my arm. I got nowhere else to be.

"Maybe halfway."

"What's left?"

"I visited the counselor at the college, and I'm signed up this fall, but it feels unresolved because I'm not sure what to do with myself, you know?"

"Maybe you should think about what you might want to do for other people?"

"What do you mean?"

"Instead of thinking about what you want to do with *you*, why don't you think about what you might want to do for someone else?"

"You don't know me." I shake my head.

"I know you a little. What about something you'd want to do that helps other people?"

Now that I think about it, his words half blow me over. What would I want to do for *other people*? I glance around the gym. This would be cool, but physical therapy is out—not just because of the one arm, but because hurting people every day isn't high on my list.

I thought about teaching, but... I don't know. "The guy at the college was pretty cool. The one who helped me with classes and stuff." But I couldn't do that. It feels huge. Grown up.

Bradley's face breaks into a smile. "I got a brother who does that. Guidance counselor."

"I could do it with one arm." I smirk. "But all the school..."

"What about helping at a high school instead of a college? You could still help with the JROTC maybe, and you could teach history—put all those hours in front of the History Channel to good use?"

I open my mouth to ask him how he knows about the History Channel, but then I remember I make him turn it on when I know I'm going to be here for a while. He came to the same conclusion I've thought about. Maybe it isn't as far out of my reach as I thought.

I start to feel lighter, but think of the years of school, and shake my head. "I don't know. It'll take forever."

Bradley laughs. "Aidan. All you got is time, man. You got

money to pay you while going to college. Money for college. You got time."

I'm still not sure. "It feels like doing nothing to me. Just going to school. Not real."

"Aidan. You don't have to be fighting a war to be doing something that counts. Think of college as your job for the next few years." Bradley leans toward me a bit. "It's your *job*."

We sit in silence as my brain wraps around all this new information. "And if I decided I wanted to teach something else—"

"It wouldn't be that big of a deal. You have a starting place now, right? And isn't that what you needed to get motivated?" Bradley slugs my good shoulder as he stands up off the mat.

"It's exactly what I needed." And for the first time since I got home, I'm actually looking forward to starting classes. The problem is that I'm further down on my list, and I'm not sure I want to be. I don't know if Kate's on my list anymore, and that last item's going to be a killer.

23

Kate Walker

With my whole turnaround, and willingness to check blood sugar and eat a healthy lunch in front of mom, I'm allowed the car. For two hours. But my hands are sweaty and slip on the steering wheel, and my heart pounds so loud I can't hear the engine. It's been two days, four text messages, and countless phone calls—all with no reply. Now I'm going to drive up and probably make a fool out of myself.

I'm also well aware that talking isn't always my strong suit, but I have to find him. I want to tell him I'm sorry and that I had this total revelation, and I want to explain why I didn't say anything. I'm sure I could say it better now than while I was coming off my low in the hospital. Make him understand.

But as I pull up between Jen's house and Aidan's apartment, I have no idea what to say. What would it be like to stand in front of him and have him still be angry with me?

Oh, God. I don't think I can do this.

My legs shake as I get out of the car and force myself up the stairs.

"Aidan's not here," Jen calls from her porch.

I spin around and feel a little guilty that I'm knocking on his door instead of hers. Equal parts relief and disappointment flow through me, making me even weaker than I was.

"Oh."

I shuffle down the stairs and toward her porch. Now I really, really want to ask where he is, but I'm almost afraid to. Did he just leave? Is he coming back? My heart starts hammering. Again.

"He said he was going to take off for a few days." She gives me a half-frown.

I flop onto her porch swing.

"Sorry, Kate, but you really freaked him out."

"I know." I run a hand over my hair.

"I can't believe your parents are letting you drive."

Me either. "Yeah, I know."

There's probably a ton I need to say to Jen, not just Aidan. I try to sort out the thoughts in my mind, but now she's looking at me like I'm crazy because I'm not saying anything. I need to *get it out*.

"I've been..." I push out air. "I've been really stupid about it. My diabetes. And I know I get frustrated with you, but I'm really going to try. And thanks for checking up on me even though you know I'm going to roll my eyes."

Jen sits next to me. We're not really touchy-feely friends, so we just sit shoulder to shoulder.

"It's okay."

"I'm going to...drive for a while I guess." And maybe do

something really pathetic like close my eyes and pretend he's sitting next to me. Well, maybe I won't close my eyes since I'm driving...

"I'll tell him you stopped by if I see him, okay?"

"Thanks, Jen." I stand. "Mom's keeping me home for a few days, but I'll be back to school, and she *always* lets you come over."

Hopefully she'll see it as the invite it is.

"I'll see you soon then." She grins as I head back to Mom's car in search of Aidan.

Next stop. His mom's house.

Christie wanders out to the porch as I pull up.

"Kate! What a surprise!" she calls as I open the car door and head her direction.

"Hi, Christie. I'm um..."

"Looking for Aidan?" She raises a brow and looks so much like Jen's mom it's spooky.

"Yeah." We now share the porch, but it's a bit awkward standing on the porch of someone's house that I barely know because I'm falling for her son who is really, really mad at me.

Her smile turns different and it's one I definitely recognize and definitely don't want to see. Sympathy.

"He's got a lot to sort out, Kate. A list of stuff. I think he needs some thinking space."

I blink back tears, but I can't keep them all in. "I didn't mean to mess up so bad."

"Oh. Kate." Her arm goes over my shoulders. "We never do."

What sucks the worst here is that she probably knows the whole story and she didn't tell me it wasn't that bad. She didn't tell me not to worry. She basically agreed with me in that I messed up bad, even though I didn't mean to.

It's not what I wanted to hear. Now I realize that what I wanted to hear was her telling me how happy Aidan will be when he knows that I've been looking for him. That he's been waiting for me to make the first move.

No such luck. She gives me a hug and I don't know if her sympathy makes the whole situation better or worse because she knows Aidan and knows I'm in need of sympathy. Maybe we can't be patched up. I back away from her thinking definitely worse. I don't even know where to go from here. "Could you—"

"I'll tell him you stopped by." She nods.

"Thanks. So much."

I step off the porch toward Mom's car and that's it. Complete and total failure. I screwed this one big time, and I don't see a fix right now.

I hurt him, and he's already dealing with too much. Why would he want to deal with me?

Deena and I are up way too late for the first time since she's been home. We're resting in bed on our stomachs, our faces together, just like when we were kids. I feel kind of bad that I haven't really taken a whole lot of time with her since she got here. With her puking so much, and me being pretty much irritated with...almost everyone, we haven't talked the way we used to.

"Still sad he hasn't called?" She tucks a chunk of hair behind my ear.

"His mom said he had a list of stuff to sort." And I'm all cried out, which is a relief because it's starting to make me feel exhausted and really pathetic.

"A list isn't a bad idea." Deena cocks a brow.

"I don't think she meant an actual list." I recognize the look in Deena's eyes, and she's so going to want to jump in on this.

"Still. Not a bad idea." The words singsong out of her mouth. And if anyone else singsonged words, I could roll my eyes. But when Deena singsongs, it's final.

"I can't even think about that. My list would be a mile long." I let my head rest deeper in my pillow.

"Like?"

"Well, I apologized to Jen today for not appreciating her more." Or something like that. "Shelton and I still have weirdness. Just thinking about Aidan makes it feel like my chest has been ripped out. I don't know what to do about college and Mom and Dad. And I hate that my doctor is all buddy-buddy with Dad. It makes me feel ganged up on."

"So find your own doctor." She bumps my shoulder with hers. "And one thing can get marked off your list."

"I can't just–"

"Why not?" Deena's eyes widen.

"I guess…" Could I? I mean I just need an endocrinologist, someone who manages people with diabetes. "Maybe I could." I'm lighter. Moving forward again. I want to share this with Aidan. Show him how I'm changing. How I'll be better. No way I'm going to voice this out loud, because Deena will give me the lecture about how I need to be doing all this for myself. One step at a time, I say. I'm at least taking charge here. A bit.

"You should try that super awesome doctor from the hospital. She works with Dad's friend, remember?"

"Yeah." She was pretty awesome. One of the few doctors I've met that looked at me instead of Mom and Dad. "But that still doesn't resolve the college issue."

"Mom and Dad want you close to home." I can't read Deena's voice, and I think she might even agree with them.

The tension builds in my chest at the thought of passing out like I did a few days ago, and not being around people who know me. Strangers. "I used to want to get away, but now I'm almost scared to, and I don't want to stay here because I'm scared."

"Kate. It's one thing to not leave home because you're afraid to not be at home. It's entirely different to be afraid because you're learning to manage your health. Maybe if you did the research on the schools close by, it won't feel like you're giving in. It'll feel like you're making a smart decision for *you*."

She's so right. I'm not sure if I'm annoyed or relieved that she figured it out. This has been a week of *really* humbling experiences.

"And you're about to be an aunt, and I like the idea of being close enough to see you once in a while." She smirks, trying to lighten the mood in the room.

"And Aidan will be here. Maybe." If he'll talk to me.

"You really fell for that guy." Deena rests her chin on her hands.

"I didn't even mean to." But the fact that I'm more hurt over losing him than I was about losing Shelton is a pretty sure sign that she's right, and I did totally fall for him. Well, me being desperate and weepy and mopey should also be a pretty fair sign of the same thing.

"You should write him a letter," Deena suggests.

"What?"

"Write him a letter. Tell him everything. Bare your soul, you know?" She giggles.

"Maybe you should do the same with Lane?" As soon as the words come out, I'm not sure if it was the right thing to say or not.

She sighs and her smile disappears. "It's not that things between us are *bad*."

"But they're not good, and you two disagree." And he left, and I know their conversations since then have been short 'cause I've been stuck in the house for most of it.

"It's not a total disagreement."

"Deena, you said he wasn't happy, and I overheard you..."

She sighs. "I can't even think about it. Him. It hurts too much. We *just* got married. This is supposed to be the time when everything's perfect."

"And it's not."

"No." She wipes a tear. "And being pregnant is making me all hormonal and crazy. I think both Lane and I are using that as an excuse as to why we're not getting along."

"Tell you what. I'll write Aidan. You write Lane." I roll onto my side to face her better.

Deena gives me a pathetic attempt at a smile. "Deal."

Crap. Now I'm going to have to actually do it.

My fingers shake as I realize I'm actually going to do this. To write him. And I'm determined to get it all out as fast as I can. And then hope I don't get a second round of rejection. At least I realize that we're both pretty far from perfect. He's disappeared on me—not nice. And I've been immature and kept things from him—also not nice. *Okay, Kate. Type already.*

Aidan,

I really hope you read this. I mean, I wouldn't blame you if you just hit delete. I get it. Everything I said or didn't say wasn't fair to you.

I found out I had diabetes when I passed out in school. Everyone knew. When I came back a week later, I was learning how to give myself shots. I had a million meetings with the nurse. I had to tell all my teachers and learn how to carry a pharmacy around with me. All my favorite foods were suddenly on a list of stuff I shouldn't eat. Or that would be so much of a pain to count carbs for that it wasn't worth it.

Everyone knew about me. There was no way for people not to know when an ambulance picked me up in the school parking lot.

I met you, and without knowing it, you understood me. You got it. And I understood you in a way that most people might not. It might not make any sense, but having a disease makes me feel gross.

I think sometimes you kind of felt that way about your arm. And so I knew you'd understand, but at the same time I was finally around someone who wasn't watching me all the time. Who wasn't looking at me for signs that my blood sugar was going too far up or down. Looking for weakness. Watching for signals that my disease was taking over. It felt like a break. Like a relief. And to be totally honest, at first you were a distraction. I totally used you to forget about everything else, and it worked.

But I don't want you to think when we spent the night together that it was about distraction. The only reason I didn't tell you I'd never had sex was because I didn't want you to treat me differently. I didn't want you to stop us. I wouldn't take the night back for anything. If you decide that you need to move past me, or that you can't deal with the crazy girl anymore, I get it. But I'm still not sorry about being with you. I will never be sorry about that.

I want to see you. Want to talk to you. When you're ready. And I hope you can understand enough to forgive me because even though you started out as a distraction, you turned into a lot more.

Kate

By the time I finish the letter, I'm in another weepy pile. Part of me knows that if this doesn't work, I've probably lost him. The worst part is that it's totally my fault.

24

AIDAN CONNELLY

Kate's letter is rattling around in my head, making me feel more than I want to, especially now.

My final big thing.

The last thing on my list.

It's just a house.

Just like every other house on the street. Only, I know better. This house isn't like any other house on the street because it holds the two people I most and least want to see in the world.

My car's in park, but the engine's still running, proving my indecision. Or maybe it's more than indecision. Maybe I'm still complete chickenshit.

No. I don't want to be. But I also don't want to face her. It's like by waiting, I've made this confrontation into a monster, rather than a really awkward afternoon. It makes me wonder if that's how Kate felt when she didn't tell me about her diabetes. Like she said in her letter—she liked having someone who didn't know. And the selfish part of me likes the idea of never being connected to Pilot again.

I should not have waited so long to come here because this is definitely going to be a bigger deal than it would have been if I'd come as soon as I got back.

I turn the car off. One more step. One more thing that brings me closer to walking up to the door. But I reach around and almost start the car again. My heart's banging in my chest, my ears. My pulse bulges in my throat. Over talking to a person.

I was in a war zone. I shot at people. People shot at me. I got my arm blown off, and now I'm worried about talking to a girl.

Pilot's girl. Not girl, wife. Pilot's *wife*. His son. Little Pilot. Jimmy. *Shit*.

I push open the car door and jog up the steps before I can change my mind. My hand reaches to knock and the door pulls open.

Melinda's standing what looks like a mile below me. She's such a tiny little thing. Her eyes water up immediately. God, I can't do this.

But it's too late. Her arms fly around me, and her face hits the center of my chest.

"God. Connelly. I was afraid I'd never see you."

I don't want this. Don't want to feel this. Face this. Not again. I take a step back, but she doesn't let me go, doesn't move her face from where it's buried in my chest.

Her words, her tight arms, the emotion comes off her, around her, breaks me. It breaks me like I didn't break when I saw him in pieces next to me in the desert. I grab her and hold her tight. As tight as I can. Like maybe if I can pull on her hard enough she'll fill the hole in my chest. My eyes squeeze tight. I don't want to cry. Not now. Not ever. This still hurts a lot worse than I thought.

The tears come even though I don't want them to, and her grip doesn't loosen. I don't know how long we stand on the porch clutched together like this, and it doesn't matter. What matters is that she probably needed this more than I did.

"Mommy!"

I push the voice away.

"Mommy! I wanna watch a show!"

Melinda's arms loosen and she takes a step back. I take my arm back and press my palm against each eye, hard. Shoving the tears back in, or wiping them away.

"Hey, Jimmy." She leans forward.

I'm afraid to look.

"This is a friend of your daddy's."

I stare at the roof over the porch. My heart rips further.

"Connelly, this is Jimmy."

I force my eyes open and stare at little Pilot. Now I know why his daddy called him that. They look exactly alike.

"You haven't seen him in a while, huh?" Melinda asks.

I nod. "Not since that big picnic before we left."

"Right. He was only two, and I swear he looks more like his daddy every day."

"Just like him." I kneel down and stare into the dark brown eyes of the little boy in front of me.

"He's almost four now."

"Hey, Jimmy." I reach my hand out.

"Where's your arm?" He points.

"Um…" I've never tried to explain to a little kid.

"He got hurt in the accident that killed your dad, sweetie." Melinda's hand touches Jimmy on the head.

"I am happy you are okay." Jimmy grins wide at me and turns to his mom.

I don't hear what else he says. How can he be glad I'm okay? His dad got killed in that "accident." A random patrol around the perimeter. One we'd done what felt like a hundred times.

Pilot would always say to me, "I'd rather shoot the shit with you than most of the other guys, and I make the damn schedule. Come on."

So late at night. Night after night, Pilot and I would walk the perimeter. I don't know if someone threw something, or if it had been planted at some point in time, but his foot touched metal, and in that split second before we heard the blast, we both knew.

And Jimmy's glad I'm okay.

He's not even four years old. That's why. He doesn't get that one of us died, and one of us didn't.

I'm shaking. I close my eyes, but that brings darkness, and darkness is too close to that night. I open my eyes, and I'm in front of this house I've driven by too many times to be casual.

"Have a seat," Melinda says. "I'll be right back."

Her voice floats through my head. I'm not sure if I want to stay here anymore. Pilot should be the guy on this porch with one arm, taking care of his family. Not me. Guy with no family. Who do I really care about? My mom. My aunt, uncle, and cousins are okay, but...

I miss Kate. That really complicates things.

"Thanks for not leaving." Melinda still blots around her eyes. "Sorry about this." She fans her face a few times. "It's been long enough that I know I won't cry like this forever, but I still cry like this a lot."

"I'm sorry. About everything. I..."

"Connelly." Her hand touches my shoulder as we sit down. "It happened. I'm glad he was next to you. That he was working with someone he looked up to..."

I shake my head. "He was my sergeant, and I..."

"And he talked about you in almost every letter. How smart you were, how he couldn't believe you weren't a college guy, an officer. He was glad to have you."

I don't even know what to think about what she's telling me. It doesn't feel like something that's real. It feels like something she came up with to make me feel better.

"So, what are you going to do with yourself?" she asks.

"Going to college. I might be a teacher, I think." It's insane to hear myself say the words out loud, but the longer I carry the decision, the better it feels.

Her bright smile widens. "So, you'll be a college boy after all then?"

"Guess so."

"And you're still in touch with the guys, right?" Her voice is quiet.

"Spent some time with Roberts, and we're going to get together again soon." We've at least talked since I walked away from him in the store.

"How's life going aside from all your new decision making?"

"I'm alive, and it's hard to be grateful for that one, simple thing when I feel like the wrong guy died." I've never said this out loud before. I've thought it in a million different ways.

Melinda looks almost confused for a moment. She sucks in a few breaths, probably trying not to cry, and this is where I want to walk away, but my body won't move.

"I could lie to you, and tell you I'm glad it was you who survived. But now that I see you here, and now that I know he's gone. Really, really, gone. I'm so glad you survived it, Connelly. You'll get to have the life he didn't." Her voice breaks again and a few tears escape.

"I'm sorry."

"A lot of people are sorry." She stares at her lap for a moment, and I'm sure I'm a jerk for wanting to take off and get out of here, but I don't know how much more I can take.

I lean forward to rest my elbows on my knees, but I only have one elbow, so I sit back up.

"You have a girl?" she asks.

Everyone's with the same questions—*How's life with one arm? What are you doing with yourself? Got a girl?*

"I...I don't know." But all I can see is Kate's smile. Hear her making some random comment about my hand, instead of hands. Or how she helped me drive my car again before I sold it. And Kate, so sure of herself taking off her shirt. Taking off my pants. Her hands. Her crying face when I walked out of the hospital.

"You do have a girl." Melinda pinches my cheek. "I'm glad."

We sit in silence for a few more moments. I'm not sure how to leave, or if I should stay or what happens now.

"It's a lot, isn't it?" She doesn't even have to explain that one.

"Yeah." I stare at my legs. She's doing the same.

"I don't want you to stay away, okay? Even though I'll probably cry again next time you come."

"Okay." I stand up. Good enough. That's enough of an invitation for me to go. "Thanks, Connelly." Her arms come around me. "Good to see you. Next time bring the girl."

She doesn't look at me again, just turns and walks back into her house.

I turn and make my way down to the car in front of the house I've driven by way too many times. Now I'll be stopping in.

Like Melinda said, the sadness won't last forever.

And that's huge.

25

Kate Walker

I sit in the empty hallway after school waiting for Jen—kind of a habit for a best friend of an overachiever. My last two days before I get my insulin pump. It feels like my last two days of freedom, even though my new doc assured me I'll feel loads better, and I won't be chained to my pharmaceutical bag.

Shelton appears next to me.

"Hey." I look up.

"Can I sit?"

I shrug and he slides to sitting. "How are things?"

"Do I look that bad?"

"A little." A corner of his mouth pulls up, and there's enough of the friend there that I know we'll talk. I'll talk.

"Just. Sometimes everything falls apart at once, you know?" And I'm slowly putting it back together, but it's taking a freaking eternity. Or maybe it feels like an eternity because I haven't talked to Aidan in over a week.

"Sorry, Kate." And he sounds it. It's not his condescending adult voice, or an I-told-you-so kind of voice.

"Thanks." I push out a breath. "I'm going to try out the insulin pump for a while."

"Big deal for you."

"I'm kind of sick just thinking about it." I clutch my stomach.

"Really?"

"You know how I am about needles." I roll my eyes.

He does this weird little half-snort, half-chuckle. "Yeah. I know. But it's not really a needle, it's a—"

"I know." And I don't want to think about that either.

"And you won't be pricking your finger all the time and giving yourself shots. I bet it'll be good once you give it a chance."

He's just being so normal and nice.

"Sorry I was snotty after our breakup."

"Sorry I wasn't smarter about the way I did it." His dark eyes are on me. "And Jen told me what happened with Aidan. As weird as it was, I'm sorry about that too."

"Thanks."

We sit in silence for a minute, and Shelton's right. We're friends. There's no fiery tingling when he sits next to me. He's just comfortable.

"Tamara and I split."

"I saw her crying."

He closes his eyes. "In the long run, I knew we'd end up being friends instead of being together. I could feel us heading there, and I was okay with that. But once we split, I didn't like the idea of being alone. I knew she liked me. It really wasn't fair to her."

"So, not the best reason to start dating someone else." And part of me would love to hear Shelton agree with me. Tell me I'm right.

"Well, you jumped right into a relationship."

Yeah, it was a long shot to think he'd admit to being wrong. He also makes an annoyingly good point.

"Because Aidan gets me." And Shelton doesn't, but I leave that out. And my words hit me again. *He gets me.*

"Sorry, Kate." He lets out a breath—resignation. "We'll stay in touch right? And it won't be weird?"

"I'll watch you conquer the world after you graduate college," I tease with narrowed eyes.

He kisses my head, and chuckles. "We'll see."

We'll see…we'll see…right now that seems to be the mantra for my entire life.

"Kate. You're all hooked up." My new doc grins wide.

Deena was right. Dr. Morris, the awesome ER doctor from the hospital, works in my regular doctor's office a day or two a week. I chose her and it feels great.

"Don't smile." I try to frown. "I may not be sticking myself with needles, but I think I deserve the break after that huge one you just used."

"Only to get your cannula in." She shakes her head. "Your frown is not going to bother me, Kate."

There's a flat, round band-aid holding the small cannula in my skin. It's weird, having this tiny box sort of connected to me.

"Your pump is wired with Bluetooth so we can monitor you."

"I know." I push out a breath—the irritated kind.

Mom and Dad are thrilled.

"You still need to eat like you're counting carbs and insulin amounts and all that." Her voice is smooth and doesn't sound like a parent lecture. This is the biggest improvement from my last doctor.

I'm still staring at the small pink box. Did someone think a girl would suddenly think it's cool because it's pink? Or is it just to lessen the blow?

I'm embarrassed to admit that the pink does make me smile. A little.

"And we'll talk about the flex one if this works out. But this one you can detach when you need to."

"But you'll know." My eyes meet hers. The Bluetooth thing and all that.

"We'll know. But I'm not your parent. And I'm not your principal. I can only help you be healthy if you work toward being healthy."

And the rest is up to me. No one has to say it. "Thanks."

"Yep." She shakes my hand. "I know your parents still want to be involved here, so here's your stack of paperwork and information they'll want to have, okay?" She hands over a large envelope.

"Okay." And it might be difficult of me, but it feels good to be the only one in the room with my doctor. I came in and did this on my own.

"Kate!" Mom jumps to standing when I step into the waiting room.

Okay. So there was no keeping them at *home*, but still. Baby steps for all of us I guess.

"That's not so bad." Dad points to the small pink box clipped onto my jeans.

"It could be worse." And that's as far as I'm willing to go right now.

And it still hits me.

Forever.

It doesn't seem so overwhelming anymore. I think it's because I'm taking control. I have my own doctor and my own notebook for my food journal. There are still some things my body's going to have a hard time adjusting to, so I'm looking out for those. But the point is that I'm doing it.

None of it's perfect, but it's all huge steps in the right direction. Now I have to find a way to get Aidan close enough so we can talk. I really want us to be talking, especially when I'm getting the rest of my life together.

26

AIDAN CONNELLY

This time around, I'm going to be extra careful and do things right. I've been in the waiting room of Kate's dad's office for an hour. Dr. Walker. It feels a bit foreign, but good. Like I'm doing a good thing. Except now I have to find the words to apologize to her dad because not only did I yell at his daughter while she was in the hospital, but I'm sure a let a few f-bombs slip, and then I disappeared.

Kate's calls should have been enough of a sign that I needed to talk to her, but over the last couple weeks, I feel like I've finally gotten on top of everything, and that's huge.

"You can come on back." The nurse waves and I leap to standing, following her through the door.

"Aidan." Kate's dad steps back as he opens his office door.

"I'd like a minute, if you have it." I resist the urge to stuff my hand in my pocket and don't fidget.

"I'm finished for the day." He gestures for me to step in.

"I know. I waited." I sit in a small chair as he walks around his desk and sits in his large leather chair.

"What can I do for you?" he asks.

"Well...uh, this seemed like a really good idea a few minutes ago." I chuckle. "I just wanted to apologize."

"For?"

"I sorta lost it at the hospital. I didn't mean to yell like that. I was scared. She didn't tell me, you know, about her diabetes, and she passed out, and I didn't know what was going on..."

He holds his hand up between us. "I wanted to wring your neck at the time, but that night was a big turning point for her."

"Oh." He's not attacking me, or telling me to keep the hell away from his daughter, so this is already going a little better than I expected.

"And I think I owe you a thank-you for helping to drill into her what we've been trying to get her to see for over a year." He leans his elbows on the desk between us.

Not at all what I was expecting. "Oh."

"I wish it would have come about in a different way, but she's going to be okay. Healthy. Because she's finally working toward it." Dr. Walker's eyes are the same brown as his daughters', and the similarities in their features make me miss her more.

I sit silent for a moment.

He lets out an odd sort of breath like he's trying to decide what to say. "I don't want to get in the middle of whatever you two have or don't have going on, but it would be really nice if you could take the time to call her."

"So, that's what I should be here to apologize for."

"You didn't need to come at all, but I'm glad you did."

"I really like her. A lot." I can't believe this is coming out of my mouth. It's like rule number one: *Don't tell the dad you're falling for his daughter. She'll never be able to leave the house.* But I can't help it. "I guess I want you to know where I stand. There was a lot of stuff I had to sort out, and I did. I'm going to school to be a high school teacher. I start this fall. It's something I'm excited about, and it took me a while to find that." Each time I say it out loud, it becomes a little more real, and like something I'm actually going to do.

He nods.

"I'd like to come by tonight or tomorrow to see her, if that's okay with you."

He smiles and leans toward me over the desk. "I have another idea."

27

Kate Walker

"Kate!" Dad calls down the hallway. "We have to leave in ten!"

"I'll be there in a minute!" It's my eighteenth birthday. I *have* to look good. Deena and I always have a party with friends at some point in time, but Mom and Dad have always done the dinner out thing. Always. No friends. Just family.

There were years when I didn't like it so much, and years like this year where I can't wait.

After Deena's letter to Lane, he drove straight here. They've been attached ever since. And because they're married, he gets to come to dinner. It's cool. Deena needs him close right now anyway.

I strut down the hall in my new black dress and heels feeling amazing. My insulin pump is practically flat against me in a tiny pocket Deena sewed in, and no one not looking for it would ever notice. No checking before we go. No double-checking for insulin and shots in my bag.

"You look so grown up." Mom's chin gets all frowny as I hit the living room.

"You're funny, Mom." I kiss her cheek, kiss the cheek

of my very stunned dad, and grin at Deena who gives me a thumb's up.

I pick up my tiny clutch, instead of my monster purse, when there's a knock at the door.

"Would you get that, Kate?" Dad asks.

Weird.

"Sure." I step around the couch and pull open the door to see Aidan. In a button-up shirt, khakis, and a tie.

"Holy shit," he whispers. "You look amazing."

I spin to see if anyone's staring (everyone is), so I step onto the porch and close the door behind me. Aidan is here. I swallow, trying to push some of my nervousness away. "What are you doing here?"

"I…" He shakes his head, making me feel again how much I've missed him. "I had it all worked out what I was going to say."

I want to hug him, throw my arms around him, but he's still thinking, and I'm still a bit unsure if he'll let me touch him again.

Aidan's here. And he looks hot. A button-up and tie suits him. "So, let's hear it." I fold my arms, but still can't hide my smile. I'm just relieved. *So* relieved. And it should be me chasing after him, but I already tried that, and maybe he got the message, bringing him to my doorstep.

"Okay. Here it is. I know that pulling a disappearing act was a shitty thing to do. Really shitty. But I got to the bottom of my list. I even went and visited Pilot's wife. I think I know what I'm doing in school. I feel good. Better than good. Better than I thought I'd ever feel again when I first came home. And so much of that had to do with you, Kate. So much of it." His eyes don't waver from mine, and he is less broken. I can see it. Feel it in his words. Whatever it is between us suddenly feels so real it takes my breath away. And maybe at this point in my life, or after my split with Shelton, my feelings should scare me, but they don't.

"I'm staying here for school," I say. "To stay with the same doctor for a bit longer. And I have one of those insulin pump things. I'm not measuring and doing shots all the time, but..." I lean closer to whisper. "I'm attached to this thing, so if you think we're going to have sex, I need a head's up."

He shakes his head again in a sort of embarrassed way and stares at the ground, his dimples showing that he's trying not to smile. "And here I was coming to tell you that I want to start all over. Do things right."

"*Really?*" I'm getting a do-over with Aidan, and it's a good thing because I can't believe I just made that sex comment.

"Yes, really." He grins. "I spent like thirty minutes buttoning this damn shirt to take you out, and Uncle Foster had to do my tie. Do you have any idea how much it sucks to have a guy do your tie?"

I try not to laugh and take a step closer.

"Well, it sucks."

"Sorry." And then I remember something. "Sorry. It's my birthday, and we always do a family thing, and..." And *I can't go out with you.* No no no no no.

"I know. Your dad invited me." He reaches out and touches the ends of my hair sending a thrill of shivers through my body.

What?

The door opens behind me, and I jump back, realizing how close Aidan and I are standing.

"We ready?" Dad asks as he gives him a nod.

"Um..." My eyes go from Aidan to my parents, and then to Deena, who's doing a lousy job of holding in her smile.

Oh. I see. "Everyone knew but me?"

Deena giggles in affirmation.

"What if I screamed and yelled and told him to go away?"

"Then we would've uninvited him," Mom says.

"Or left you at home," Dad teases as he rubs his hand across my shoulders. "Why don't you jump in with Aidan, and we'll see you two there."

Whoa. "Okay."

My parents climb into their car as Aidan takes my hand. Even this feels significant.

I follow Aidan to his car in a bit of a daze and sit. As soon as he gets in his side of the car, there's something I have to say. "I like you, and I sort of lose my head when we're together, and I expected too much of you, and jumped in too fast, but I really, really like you."

"Kate." He smirks.

"What?"

"You're about to say something crazy."

I laugh. "Probably."

"Go ahead." He twists his body and runs his fingers up my arm, stealing my thoughts for a moment.

"I'm sorry I didn't say anything. Sometimes I feel like it would be easier if I was missing an arm, and hiding the truth wasn't an option. I should have trusted you with everything."

"I had stuff to sort out too, Kate. And I did. Better we ran into this mess sooner and not later, right?" He inches closer.

Sooner instead of later. Because he wants us to have a later. "You're sorted?"

"More of a work in progress."

"Perfect, so am I."

We sit in silence for a moment. His blue eyes locked with mine. This is it. He's it. My heart's wild, but in a way that makes me feel like this is real. And I'm still the girl I used to be, but I'm also so much more.

Aidan leans in, and his soft kiss melts every part of me, and this is nothing of what we were a couple weeks ago. This is who we are now. And who we will be. Together.

Acknowledgments

I have to thank my husband first because the moment I told him about Aidan's backstory, he looked at me and said, "Yes. You have to write this book." Even more props to him because I'm pretty sure I woke him up to tell him about it...

A huge thanks to Nyrae Dawn for tweeting about her favorite part, which may have involved a particular night between my two main characters, creating a stream of tweets begging to read the scene. And to my fab friends—Christa and Rhiannon—for reading the scene and also saying, "Yes. Finish this book. Get it into the world. And can I read it when you're done?"

For my other awesome readers, authors Cassie Mae and Morgan Shamy, you boost my ego and I love you for it. And to Heidi Willis, my diabetic expert, you rock. My grandma didn't live to tell me about her life with the disease, so I'm glad I had you.

Major thank-yous to the lovely people at Albert Whitman. They created a cover that captured the feeling of the book perfectly and have been nothing but delightful to work with. Also to my editor,

Wendy McClure, I bow to your awesomeness. Editing made me love this story more, not less, and that's a fabulous thing.

After my husband's time in the military, I have such a huge appreciation for what our servicemen and -women do. We are truly in your debt. And thank you to the Wounded Warrior Project, an organization that moves mountains for people—or gives them the tools to move mountains on their own. Without your existence, I would not have finished this book.

Don't miss these great reads from Jolene Perry!

Available now...

Stronger Than You Know • 978-0-8075-3155-6 • $16.99

Joy's years with her abusive mother are now behind her. But now, in her new life, she has a whole list of reasons why she's crazy. Will she ever truly belong in a world that seems too normal to be real?

"A moving survival story."—*Booklist*

"Complex characters and a well-structured plot...Joy's story is very affecting."—*Kirkus Reviews*

"While the subject matter is tough, this realistic title will draw teens in with its believable characters."—*School Library Journal*

Coming soon...

HAS TO BE LOVE

978-0-8075-6557-5 • $16.99

*Read on for a special preview
of the irresistible new novel from Jolene Perry!*

In her small Alaskan town, Clara's used to the kind of looks she gets
from having scars on her face. It's a different story when it comes
to strangers. One of them, though, a student teacher in her English
class, is the first person to really understand her dream of going to
New York and being a writer. Yet Clara's plans for the future also
involve Elias, the guy who's always been there for her, and who says
he wants forever. And then nothing truly seems possible until she
gets surgery that will fix her face.

But life doesn't always follow a plan...

III

Rhodes follows me up the trail on the edge of the forest to the wooden barn behind the house. I wipe my sweaty palms on my pants and try to take a deep breath. I'm seriously being ridiculous. Totally ridiculous. Like girls who swoon over boy-bands ridiculous. He's an older guy that I just met. That's all.

"So, do you guys stay up all night in the summer?" he asks. "Because of the light?"

"Sometimes." I'm not sure how different it could possibly be just because it's light.

His gaze scans the tall trees around us. The path to the barn is wide enough for two cars to go side by side, but it is still cut through the trees, giving it a kind of private feeling.

"Do you worry about bears?"

My answer gets stuck in my throat before sort of coughing out. "Yep. Especially this time of year."

His eyes begin to scan more thoroughly.

"Where are you from?" I ask. Totally safe question.

"Everywhere. My dad is career Air Force. I was born in Germany and spent most of my childhood there. We were in Italy for a while and then moved back to the states when I was in high school. California."

So many places. In seventeen years, I've been here and to Seattle. "Wow."

"It's given me a severe case of wanderlust, which is why I'm up here."

Wanderlust is something I only half understand. Going to Seattle still feels like another world. "Oh."

I tap my back pocket. Notebook still there. But the double-check gives me something to do while nerves ball up in my throat.

After I slide open the large barn door and step inside, Snoopy sticks his black and white head over the stall door, shoving his nose into my face. Our two horses are in box stalls—more like fenced-in areas inside the barn. I've always loved how open it is.

"So, is everyone up here into the outdoor stuff? Do you have a raft? Or do you know someone who could take me down the river? Is it too cold to swim? Can we fish on the river, or is that just certain times of the year?"

I let out a slight laugh. "I'm not really sure what to answer first."

"Sorry," he says as he follows me into the barn. "I really want to experience being here you know?"

No, I don't know. "Yes, tons of people have rafts. Elias has a really nice one. We only jump into the river briefly. The current is strong enough to keep you under with or without a lifejacket. It's also hypothermia in minutes because the river is glacier fed. And fishing doesn't open on our river until sometime in July I think, but lakes are always open."

"The canyon here is deep," he says. "I guess I should have expected the glacier thing."

"We can hike that, too, if you want." What am I saying? Did I just offer to take my teacher out?

"The glacier?" he asks.

"It's not nearly as cool as it sounds. The places where you can hike to it, it's covered in dirt. I mean, we can get up onto the snow and ice, but it gets dangerous fast. There's a zip-line place up the highway, too. It's pretty fun unless you're afraid of heights."

"So. Wild. Hiking on a glacier. And for sure yes to the zip-lining." His smile widens and his eyes are on me for another minute before he scans the inside of the barn. Rhodes eyes follow the same trail that everyone's do. Around the bottom floor, with the horse stalls and tack room. Then his gaze travels up to the loft, which is half open to below, allowing the smell of hay to permeate the barn. He looks a lot more like a student than a teacher in this moment.

"This is cool," he says. "I'm sorry. My thoughts are all over the place. I love being somewhere new."

I can't imagine loving being somewhere new, but maybe with a new face that'll feel simpler too.

I measure out the grain in the large can and start dumping it in buckets. Keeping busy around someone my body's reacting to, is probably smart. "Dad built it with Mom when I was a baby. Just after building the house."

"You've lived here a long time."

"My whole life."

"You're going to college, right?" He leans against Snoopy's stall, and my horse immediately shoves his nose in Rhodes' hand. He grabs Snoopy's upper lip, and tugs, playing my horse's favorite game.

"Why do you ask?" I grab a few flakes of hay and start tossing them over the tops of the stalls, wondering where Rhodes was when he got acquainted with horses.

"My experience says that it's really good for us to get out of our comfort zone once in a while. And if you wanna be a writer, like my aunt said, I don't think you'll get the teaching you need up here."

I want to be a writer.

It's the thing, the career, the drive that feels fragile—like if it's talked about too much or hoped for too much, it'll shatter before I have a chance for it to begin. At the same time, I can't imagine something so…foreign or something so incredible. At least not yet.

"I might go up to UAF for my freshman year," I say as I toss the last load of hay over and lean against the stall next to Rhodes. University of Alaska is a massive compromise, but it's one I'm willing to make to stay close to home—at least until my scars are fixed, then the world might seem less like a cliff I've been asked to climb with no gear. That's when I'll maybe leave for New York, but not before. I'm still not sure how to manage the idea of leaving Elias behind for Columbia. I shove the thought away.

His brow furrows. "You might want to think about somewhere else. See the world a little. I fully believe in current opportunity."

"What does that mean?" I ask.

"It means that life is too short to wait for things to come to you." He gives me a purposefully crooked smile, like he thinks he's cute or something. "Sometimes you have to reach out and try for what you want. Sometimes you don't know what you want until it's right in front of you. I had no idea I wanted to go to Alaska until my aunt suggested it, and now here I am, experiencing Alaska."

I'm self-aware enough to know I hide in my bubble, but that's as temporary as my scars.

I trace the welts coming off my upper lip as I lean against Snoopy's stall.

Rhodes' eyes are on me. Something in me should be squirming under his gaze because we just met, but there's an odd sense of old soul that makes me feel like I've known him longer than I have.

People don't normally warm up to me like this. They always keep their distance for a while, watch me, and wait to feel comfortable before they talk. It's one of the things I love about Knik—everyone here knows me, and knows the story of my scars. I get second glances, but not the stares I get when I'm somewhere new.

Jolene Perry grew up in south central Alaska. She has lived in a cabin on a lake island, sailed the Bahamas, taught middle school and high school, and she married the guy she kissed on her high school graduation night. Her books include *Out of Play, Stronger Than You Know,* and *Has to Be Love.* Jolene lives with her husband and two children in Alaska. Visit her online at **jolenebperry.com**.